Poetry of the First World War

Notes by Hana Sambrook

Longman

York Press

YORK PRESS
322 Old Brompton Road, London SW5 9JH

Pearson Education Limited
Edinburgh Gate, Harlow,
Essex CM20 2JE, United Kingdom
Associated companies, branches and representatives throughout the world

First published 1997
Eleventh impression 2006

ISBN-10: 0-582-31453-4
ISBN-13: 978-0-582-31453-5

Illustrated by Robert Loxston
Designed by Vicki Pacey, Trojan Horse
Timeline by Vicki Pacey, Trojan Horse
Phototypeset by Gem Graphics, Trenance, Mawgan Porth, Cornwall
Colour reproduction and film output by Spectrum Colour
Produced by Pearson Education Asia Limited, Hong Kong

Contents

Preface

York Notes are designed to give you a broader perspective on works of literature studied at GCSE and equivalent levels. We have carried out extensive research into the needs of the modern literature student prior to publishing this new edition. Our research showed that no existing series fully met students' requirements. Rather than present a single authoritative approach, we have provided alternative viewpoints, empowering students to reach their own interpretations of the text. York Notes provide a close examination of the work and include biographical and historical background, summaries, glossaries, analyses of characters, themes, structure and language, cultural connections and literary terms.

If you look at the Contents page you will see the structure for the series. However, there's no need to read from the beginning to the end as you would with a novel, play, poem or short story. Use the Notes in the way that suits you. Our aim is to help you with your understanding of the work, not to dictate how you should learn.

York Notes are written by English teachers and examiners, with an expert knowledge of the subject. They show you how to succeed in coursework and examination assignments, guiding you through the text and offering practical advice. Questions and comments will extend, test and reinforce your knowledge. Attractive colour design and illustrations improve clarity and understanding, making these Notes easy to use and handy for quick reference.

York Notes are ideal for:
- Essay writing
- Exam preparation
- Class discussion

The author of these Notes is Hana Sambrook. Hana was educated at the Charles University in Prague and the University of Edinburgh. She worked as an editor in educational publishing and was for some years on the staff of Edinburgh University Library. Now a freelance editor in London, she is the author of several York Notes, including Sylvia Plath's *Selected Works*.

Health Warning: **This study guide will enhance your understanding, but should not replace the reading of the original text and/or study in class.**

PART ONE

INTRODUCTION

HOW TO STUDY A POEM

You have bought this book because you wanted to study the poets of the First World War on your own. This may supplement work done in class.

- Reading poetry is quite different from reading a novel or a play. There is no story, or 'plot', to urge you to read on, to see what happened next. (In some of the war poems a story may be hinted at, but there is no element of surprise: the outcome is invariably death.)
- Instead of a cast of characters there is the poet and you, the reader. This is a one-to-one relationship in which you have to try to share the emotions that inspired the poem and are expressed by the poet indirectly, through imagery and rhythm.
- The form of a poem is important, and you must consider the poet's choice of words with care. It is hard work, but rewarding for the pleasure of discovering the meaning of the images used and, at the same time, realising both their accuracy and their beauty.
- Because of the one-to-one relationship between the writer and the reader, poetry is particularly suited for study on your own.
- Write down your impressions of a poem after your first reading, with a note of the book in which the poem is to be found and of the page number. Reread your notes later. Have your views changed? How? Through your reading of other poems or through reading the commentaries?
- The comments on individual poems in the Summaries section (pp. 13–51) should be read *after* your first reading of the poems. You may find these comments reassuring (if you agree) or challenging (if

you disagree). Either way, they should help you to formulate your own views and ideas.

- Some knowledge of the background (see Context & Setting, pp. 8–12) may change your estimation of a poem.

Studying on your own requires self-discipline and a carefully thought-out work plan to be effective.

CONTEXT & SETTING

THE HISTORICAL BACKGROUND

War declared The First World War was triggered off by the assassination in Sarajevo on 28 June 1914 of Archduke Franz Ferdinand of Austria by a Serbian nationalist. Austria accused Serbia of involvement in the murder and declared war. Germany joined in, declaring war first on Russia, the champion of all Slavs, and later on France, Russia's ally. German armies invaded Belgium as the shortest route to France, and England came in, bound by a treaty with Belgium. So the battle lines were drawn up: the Allies (Britain, France, Russia, Serbia and later Japan) against the Central Powers (Germany, Austria-Hungary, Turkey and later Bulgaria).

The two sides were now fighting in Belgium and eastern France. Instead of a swift victory, predicted by both sides, the opposing armies settled down to trench warfare, advancing and retreating, always with heavy casualties.

A modern war? This was the first war in which modern weapons were used. The tank was invented by the British in 1916, and the Germans introduced poison gas a year earlier. Aeroplanes and airships were also used, though on a small scale and largely for reconnaissance. Yet the war

was largely fought by infantrymen using rifles, bayonets and hand grenades, in the trenches – that underground network of passages that became muddy, waterlogged and bitterly cold for months on end.

Causes of the war

The assassination in Sarajevo had triggered off the war. Yet, can the murder of one man, even the heir to the Austrian throne, offer an adequate explanation for carnage on such a vast scale? Almost 8.5 million men were killed, and vast numbers of others were wounded, blinded, gassed and driven to insanity by what they had seen.

With hindsight we can say that the assassination was an excuse, eagerly seized by Germany, with Austria following her lead. Germany had been spoiling for war ever since her victory over France in 1870. She was a militaristic nation, and her ambitions could only find expression in war. She wanted not only her share of overseas colonies, but also the resulting industrial and commercial benefits of colonialism. She also wanted better access to the overseas markets than her ports on the North and Baltic Seas provided. She was hungry for expansion in Europe as well, especially to the East (*Drang nach Osten* – the drive eastward).

There were other factors contributing to the eagerness for war.

- There was the restless mood of small European nations resentful of the Germanising and Russifying policies of their masters.
- Many patriots saw in the war a chance of breaking the rigid political order and gaining freedom for their countries.

Apart from Britain whose army at the outbreak of the war consisted of professional soldiers and volunteers, all the major European countries had huge armies of conscripted men just waiting to be used (Britain introduced compulsory military service in 1916). With vast armies at their disposal it seemed natural to the generals on both sides to use them.

In addition, the system of alliances between nations – ironically, formed in fear of war – ensured that the war spread throughout Europe. It seems to us now that people simply could not believe that they were creating such a hell, and so they made no effort to stop it.

War as madness

A number of reasons for the outbreak of the war have been put forward here. In the end, however, it can only be seen as a monstrous act of collective madness, described by Robert Graves in *Recalling War* as 'an infection of the common sky', a war hysteria that spread like a plague throughout Europe and beyond.

ENGLAND IN 1914

The Edwardian era – roughly the first decade of the twentieth century leading up to the war - has been recalled in fiction and biography with nostalgic affection for those golden years.

In England it was, of course, a very pleasant time to live, if you happened to have been born into the comfortable middle class or the aristocracy. Food was cheap (imported from the colonies), taxes were low, domestic labour was cheap and plentiful, and life was agreeable.

The rigid class system seemed set in place, unquestioned because there was no real sense of social justice, instead of which there was charitable work carried out as a social duty by middle-class women. There was security in such unquestioning acceptance of the social order, and the placidity of the political scene was reflected in the literature of the period. The writers and their readership shared the same moral and aesthetic values, decent if a little dull.

The plight of the working class

If you belonged to the working class, however, things were quite different. There was no proper Health Service, no adequate old age or disability pension, only elementary education (provided free after 1870), and work was not always easy to find. The armies of servants that made life so easy for the privileged were willing to work for low wages because the alternative was starvation. (You might almost say, only half as a joke, that the lavish use of servants acted as a welfare system of sorts.)

The working class was still of little account politically, and we might be allowed to wonder whether there was a link between this disregard of a large section of the population, and the generals' readiness to waste soldiers' lives in such large numbers simply to test out badly planned strategies.

The poets of the war

It took the war to bring the privileged young men into real contact with working men. The young officers who volunteered for the the army in the first flush of patriotic zeal (and whose life expectancy was soon to be reckoned in months rather than years) came to care for the men under their command, and to share their dislike of the High Command, that was so smug, well behind the line of fire.

Most of the poets of the war came from similar comfortable, civilised backgrounds. They were 'officer material', with few exceptions educated at public schools and Oxbridge. Their idealism, grounded in the Hellenic ideals of their classical education, could not survive the reality of the trenches. Instead, these poets found their inspiration in their pity for the men under their command, and ultimately in their fierce, bitter anger.

Part two

Summaries

A note on the text

The poems discussed here can be found in the anthologies listed below: all are currently available, most of them in paperback editions. The three anthologies marked* contain the fullest selection of the poems discussed. The punctuation, spelling and grammar used in quotations are based on the most popular anthologies.

The alphabet letter preceding each title in the list below is also used in the Summaries to indicate in which anthologies a poem may be found.

The same system is used in the Commentary section, after the title of any additional poem referred to in the Commentary but not discussed in the Summaries, to enable the student to locate it.

(G) GARDNER, B. (Ed.) *Up the Line to Death: The War Poets 1914–1918*, Methuen, London, 1964, reissued 1986

(K) KITCHEN, D. (Ed.) *Axed between the Ears: a Poetry Anthology*, Heinemann Educational, London, 1987

(M) MARTIN, C. *War Poems*, Unwin Hyman, London, 1990, Collins Educational, London, 1991

*(C) PARSONS, I.M. (Ed.) *Men who March Away: Poems of the First World War*, Chatto, London, 1965

(R) REILLY, C.S. (Ed.) *Scars Upon My Heart: Women's Poetry and Verse of the First World War*, Virago, London, 1981

*(P) SILKIN, J. (Ed.) *The Penguin Book of First World War Poetry*, Penguin, Harmondsworth, 1971

*(O) STALLWORTHY, J. (Ed.) *The Oxford Book of War Poetry*, Oxford University Press, Oxford, 1984

Edmund Blunden (1896–1974)

Biography

Edmund Blunden was educated at Christ's Hospital, Horsham and (after the war) at Queen's College, Oxford. He volunteered in 1916 and survived the terrible battles of the Somme, Ypres and Passchendaele, winning the Military Cross. His post-war career was devoted to teaching English literature in Tokyo, and later at Oxford, and to writing. His work reflects his two lifelong preoccupations: his love of the southern English landscape and his compulsion to bear constant witness to the horrors of the war, as if to atone for having survived when so many did not.

As well as in verse, he recorded his war experiences in a moving prose memoir, *Undertones of War* (1928). His pity for the dead speaks throughout the book.

THE ZONNEBEKE ROAD (C/P/O)

Have the images of icy winter any other function than that of description?

The soldiers are returning from night watch, frozen to the marrow. The dull winter morning mirrors the men's mood of dull despair. They hope for nothing, and their disdain for death gives them strength.

COMMENT

Though the poem employs a formal rhyme scheme, it is a random record of thoughts passing through the poet's mind as, with his men, he stumbles back to the dugout, greeting each ghastly landmark along the way.

There is a dissonance (see Literary Terms), perhaps deliberate, between the jingling rhymes and the grim subject matter.

GLOSSARY

Haymarket the soldiers jokingly named parts of the trenches after streets in London and other British cities

Ypres there were three battles of Ypres, and there was continuous fighting in between as well

screaming dumbness this figure of speech, bringing together two contrasting terms, is called an oxymoron (see Literary Terms)

VLAMERTINGHE: PASSING THE CHÂTEAU (JULY 1917) (C/P/O)

The poem closes with a sarcastic comment.

On their way to battle the soldiers are passing château gardens in full bloom, and the poet asks ironically if they should not be garlanded with flowers like the sacrificial animals of pagan times.

COMMENT

The poem opens with a quotation from John Keats's *Ode on a Grecian Urn* describing just such a sacrificial scene depicted on a Greek vase, which draws our attention to the underlying parallel of the sacrifice of human lives in battle.

Violent death is referred to indirectly in the last line: the dull red is that of dried blood.

GLOSSARY

gone West been killed

lowing bellowing like cattle (a reminder of Keats's sacrificial beasts)

1916 SEEN FROM 1921 (C/P)

This is Blunden's fullest declaration of what the war had done to him. He sees himself as dead or wounded, dragging out his life back home, a stranger among his neighbours who do not know what the war was like.

Think of the symbolic meaning of the contrasting landscapes.

The landscape he sees most clearly is that of the battlefield, and his memory clings to moments of happiness snatched from the misery of the war.

COMMENT

No-one else has described so clearly, and so honestly, the lasting effect of war experiences on a soldier who survived. Blunden retained his sanity (unlike, for instance, Ivor Gurney, another war poet who loved the countryside), but he paid his price in his alienation from the people back home, even from his beloved

English landscape. His memories of snatched moments of happiness from the war are the most vivid.

GLOSSARY

none's at home in vain nobody is waiting for someone who will never return

shrewd sharply

RUPERT BROOKE (1887–1915)

BIOGRAPHY

Educated at Rugby School, Brooke won a scholarship to King's College, Cambridge. He had a brilliant undergraduate career which ended disappointingly with a Second Class degree in his English Tripos.

Nevertheless he seemed set on a successful academic career, writing his dissertation on John Webster, the Jacobean dramatist. He was also writing poetry and published his *Poems* in 1911.

He went through an unhappy love affair at this time and embarked on worldwide travels to forget it, putting aside his academic pursuits.

When the war broke out he joined the Royal Naval Division. On the way to Gallipoli with his ship in 1915 he died on the island of Skyros of blood poisoning caused by a mosquito bite. Like Lord Byron who also went to war for idealistic reasons (to help liberate Greece from the Turks) and died of marsh fever before he ever saw any fighting, Brooke did not die in battle.

He was a legend during his years at Cambridge and his literary reputation soared after the publication in 1914 of his five *1914* sonnets (two of which are discussed below). Their popularity was due to a considerable extent to their matching exactly the patriotic, enthusiastic mood of the time.

Most critics now believe that if he had lived through the war, Brooke would have changed his style as well as his themes. Another war poet, Charles Hamilton Sorley (who was killed in 1915) identified a basic weakness of Brooke's *1914* sonnets, saying that Brooke was 'far too obsessed with his own sacrifice'. In other words, in Brooke's eyes it was his own great worth that made his sacrifice so great.

Putting aside his soaring and falling reputation, you should read his poems for themselves: you may find them unexpectedly rewarding.

PEACE (G/M/C/O)

No poems of this sort were written at the beginning of the Second World War. Why?

The poet rejoices in the God-given chance to prove his worth in the war. It will be a new, clean, honourable life which will bring peace of mind. There will be pain and death, but all that will pass.

COMMENT

The poem was popular at the time of its publication because of its enthusiasm and its ignorance of the reality of war. For us now it is difficult to accept its rhetoric as well as the sentiments it expresses, but it repays careful reading because it describes a state of mind shared by many young men then – they saw in the war a chance to escape from their boringly safe lives as well as a chance to prove themselves (see England in 1914 on page 10).

GLOSSARY

that has ending that will stop

the worst friend ... Death see the Bible, I Corinthians 15:20, 'The last enemy that shall be destroyed is death'. The echoes of biblical language are deliberate and part of the rhetoric

THE SOLDIER (P/O)

Make a list of the emotions this poem draws on.

This is Brooke's best-known and best-loved poem, perhaps because in it he was writing his own epigraph. There is also a moving sense of the poet's deep love of England and its people.

COMMENT

The poem is often compared with Thomas Hardy's *Drummer Hodge*, written earlier, during the Boer War. Both poems share the same theme, the death and burial of a young soldier far from home, but the treatment here is quite different, as Hardy comes closer to the harsh realities of war.

ROBERT GRAVES (1895–1985)

BIOGRAPHY

Educated at Charterhouse School and, after the war, at Oxford, Graves saw service with the Royal Welch Fusiliers, was shot through the head and lungs and erroneously reported dead. He survived and during his convalescence met another war poet, Siegfried Sassoon, who was to remain a close friend for many years.

Unfit for military service, Graves left the army and after his marriage to Nancy Nicholson he went up to Oxford. He left without a degree and took up an academic post in Cairo. During his time there he wrote his autobiography, *Goodbye to All That*, judged by many to be the best account of the war.

His reputation established, he now embarked on a literary career, writing novels, poetry and works on religious, mythological and anthropological subjects. It should be noted that he excluded almost all his war poems from the later editions of his poetry.

TWO FUSILIERS (G/C)

Can you see any homosexual elements in Graves's poem?

Two friends from the Fusiliers battalion congratulate themselves on having survived the war. Their friendship was cemented by the dangers they had gone through together. Having survived, they feel more alive for having witnessed other men's death.

COMMENT

It has been suggested that the two Fusiliers are Graves himself and Siegfried Sassoon (who also served in the Royal Welch Fusiliers though not in Graves's battalion). If so, there is irony in the poem: Sassoon objected to some passages in *Goodbye to All That* (especially to Graves's remarks about Wilfred Owen), and their friendship,'so closely bound', did not survive.

GLOSSARY

Fribourt, Festubert villages in Flanders much fought over in the war

Picard clay the muddy trenches in Picardy in eastern France

RECALLING WAR (C/P/O)

Compare this poem with Blunden's 1916 seen from 1921.

The war is just a memory now, the wounds ache sometimes, the crippled men are getting used to their handicaps. Graves recalls the wartime madness, the hysterical patriotism, as well as the young men's frantic enjoyment of the pleasures on offer. The poem closes with a sardonic view of the war as a game for thoughtless children.

COMMENT

The tone is one of fastidious restraint; all the emotions are held firmly under control, and expressed in short, clipped sentences.

Sassoon once said that Graves seemed to be standing at attention when reading his poetry aloud – perhaps this habit of self-command dictates the form of the poem.

The poet allows himself the use of sarcasm, however, especially in the last stanza which ends on a sombre note of warning for the future.

GLOSSARY

silvered covered with a shiny new skin

fate-spasm the moment of death

earth to ugly earth an echo of the burial service of the Church of England, with the word 'ugly' introducing the reality of the trenches

Identify the speaker.

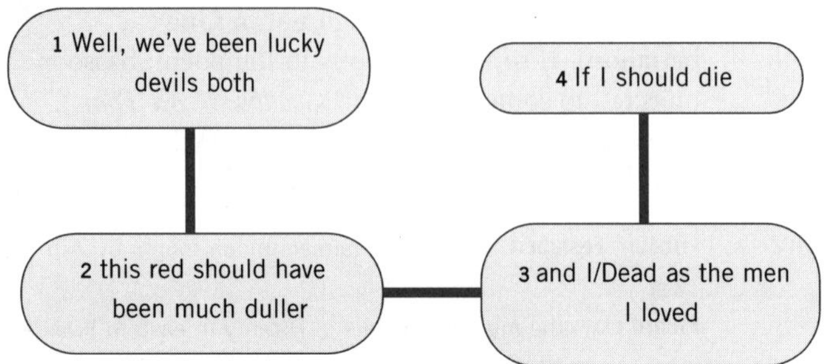

Identify the person 'to whom' this comment refers.

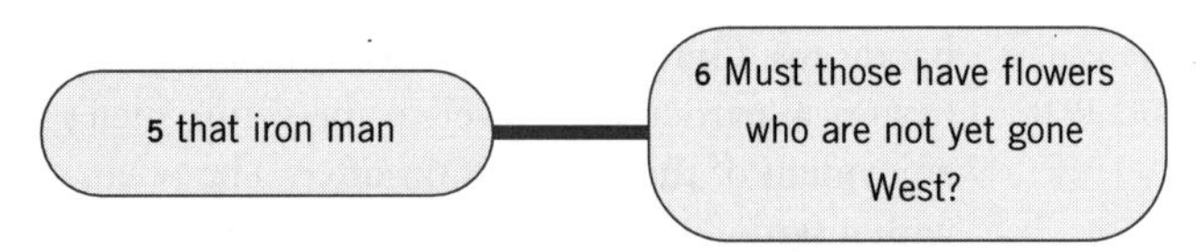

Check your answers on page 73.

Consider these issues.

a Blunden's happiest moments in the war.

b 'A word of rage in lack of meat, wine, fire' – what Graves tells us here about his bold young officers, especially about their language.

c The lack of ordinary spoken English in Brooke's *1914* sonnets, and the change of style and diction that took place as the war went on.

d Examples of the vividness of Blunden's wartime memories in his poetry.

e What you think Graves means by 'an infection of the common sky' in *Recalling War.*

f What takes the place of images of war in Brooke's *1914* sonnets.

Julian grenfell (1888–1915)

Biography

The eldest son of Lord Desborough, Julian Grenfell was educated at Eton and Balliol College, Oxford. A rarity among the war poets, Grenfell was a professional soldier, and had served in India and South Africa. His distinguished military career in France (he was awarded the Distinguished Service Order and twice mentioned in dispatches) was cut short when he died of wounds early in 1915. His younger brother Billy, a poet and scholar, was killed two months later, the Desborough title thus becoming extinct.

Into battle (M/C/P/O)

Though written in Flanders, the poem is set in a green, essentially English landscape. It is not about fighting the Germans, it is about fighting as a noble, almost mystical sacrifice, offered joyfully. In death the soldier will enter the fellowship of trees and woodland birds, welcomed by the constellations in the sky as they had welcomed the dead heroes of Greek legends.

Try to pinpoint the difference between this poem and C.H. Sorley's All the Hills and Vales Along.

Grenfell hardly speaks of the coming battle itself, the 'brazen frenzy', anticipating instead the 'joy of battle', almost welcoming death.

Into Battle is one of the most anthologised poems of the First World War.

Comment

The poem is an oddity. Enthusiastically received, it really has no place among the patriotic outpourings of the time, and once the horrors of the trenches became known, *Into Battle* became an anachronism.

Yet it is not to be mocked: deeply felt and well written, it should perhaps be seen as a curious fruit of classical education and compared to Brooke's *1914* sonnets.

GLOSSARY

has increase gains (see the Bible, I Corinthians 3:6, 'God gave the increase')

the Dog-Star Sirius, the brightest of all stars

the Sisters Seven the constellation of the Pleiades

Orion's Belt a constellation of seven bright stars
joy of battle the Norsemen had a name for this feeling – *berserk*

IVOR GURNEY (1890–1937)

BIOGRAPHY

Gloucestershire-born, the son of a tailor, Gurney was educated as a chorister at the High School, Gloucester, and won an Open Scholarship to the Royal College of Music in London. From early on he wrote poetry as well as composing music, especially songs.

Because of his weak eyesight he had some difficulty in joining up at the outbreak of the war, but finally succeeded in 1915. In 1917 he took part in the Somme offensive, was wounded, recovered and was then gassed and invalided out. In the same year he published a collection of poems, *Severn and Somme*, and composed some music as well, but by 1918 it was clear that his war experiences had affected his already fragile mental state. In 1922 he was committed to an asylum in Gloucester, and the rest of his life was spent in such institutions, some of it in the anguished belief that the war was still going on. At some time in the last years of his life he wrote a letter to the London Metropolitan Police which ends, heartrendingly: 'Asking for Death, Release or Imprisonment. And end to pain.'

TO HIS LOVE (C/P/O)

The poem starts on a quiet elegiac note, remembering past happy times back home with the friend who is now lying dead. In the last stanza the poet's anguish is expressed on a rising note of hysteria as he tries to blot out from his memory the hideous sight of his friend's mangled body.

COMMENT

Gurney's love of the Gloucestershire countryside and his love for his friend are the poem's two themes, as they are of much of the poetry of the First World War (see Themes on Love and Friendship and on Nature).

GLOSSARY

memoried remembered from the past

THOMAS HARDY (1840–1928)

BIOGRAPHY

Born at Bockhampton, Dorset, the son of a stonemason, Hardy started out as an architect, specialising in church restoration work. Soon he turned to literature, writing novels, short stories, and, in his later years, poetry. He became the foremost literary figure of his time, creating his own England, the fictional Wessex, to serve as a background to his novels.

His work seems to belong among the great nineteenth-century classics, and it may come as a surprise to find him among the war poets, but he has earned his place there. *Channel Firing* (P), written in April 1914, is a strange prophetic vision of the war to come. His masterly short poem *In Time of 'The Breaking of Nations'*, written in 1915, again looks towards the future, to peace and prosperity, and forgetting.

DRUMMER HODGE (M/P/O)

Why do you think Hardy stresses the 'Strange stars'?

Written in 1899 during the Boer War (Britain's last imperialist war), the poem has no overt pacifist message, yet it conveys quite clearly the callous waste of young lives in war. Drummer Hodge died in South Africa, in a faraway land, for a cause he did not understand, and his body, flung carelessly into his grave, will nourish the alien African soil.

COMMENT

The poem invites comparison with Rupert Brooke's *The Soldier*, especially in the last stanza. Where Brooke proudly appropriates a patch of foreign soil as 'forever England' because *he* lies buried there, poor Hodge's body in an unmarked grave will feed the African soil.

Written well before the First World War, the poem nevertheless prepares the ground for the anti-war poetry of the War.

GLOSSARY

Hodge the name was probably chosen deliberately: 'Hodge' is a nickname for the typical English countryman

kopje top of a low hill

veldt open grass country

Karoo a South African treeless plateau

A WIFE IN LONDON (DECEMBER 1899) (M)

Think about the function of the fog in this sad little poem.

Another poem written during the Boer War, but the feelings it expresses hold true for any war. A soldier's wife in London receives a War Office telegram telling her of her husband's death in battle in South Africa. The next day a letter arrives from the dead man, full of his joyful anticipation of his return to her.

COMMENT

This sad story is presented in a flat tone, offering no expression of sympathy, and apparently demanding none.

No comment is made on the late arrival of the cheerful letter, surely one of Hardy's 'Life's Little Ironies'.

GLOSSARY

whom the worm now knows who is now dead and buried

in highest feather in a very optimistic mood

IN TIME OF 'THE BREAKING OF NATIONS' (1915) (G/C/O)

Is the poem memorable because of the clear pictures it evokes or because of its message?

This is a timeless picture of peace: a man working in the field, getting it ready for sowing (and for future prosperity), a heap of weeds is smouldering near by. A pair of lovers walk by; such things go on forever.

COMMENT

This is an outstanding poem; the three small pictures of the countryside (not unlike the tiny drawings in a medieval Book of Hours) convey a powerful message.

The message is perhaps reassuring – wars always come to an end – but also oddly disturbing, for if wars are unimportant what of the lives wasted for nothing? The implied message is typical of Hardy's belief in a cruel, unfeeling and indifferent fate ruling over men's lives.

GLOSSARY

'The Breaking of Nations' see the Bible, Jeremiah 51:20, 'With thee will I break in pieces the nations', threatening the destruction of Israel's enemies

Dynasties successions of kings from the same families. The word has a special meaning for Hardy; his three-part epic drama on Napoleon is entitled *The Dynasts*

wight (*archaic*) man

A.P. HERBERT (1890–1971)

BIOGRAPHY

A.P. Herbert served at Gallipoli in Turkey and in France until invalided out. After the war he made his reputation as a humorist, a regular contributor to *Punch* and an author of witty libretti for musicals. He represented Oxford University in Parliament for many years, always a voice of common sense.

BEAUCOURT REVISITED (C)

Consider the effect of the author's use of the names of dead men and of the nicknames of places in the trenches.

The poet returns later in the war to the scene of earlier fierce fighting where many of his comrades had died. The front has moved far ahead, and there is peace round Beaucourt now. The troops marching through on their way to the front do not know what had happened here, but the dead in their graves remember.

COMMENT

The poem is unusual in that it recalls past fighting while the war is still going on, and the Allied armies have advanced farther. For the poet the village is haunted, his memories of past battles are still vivid, while the new troops passing through hardly notice the graves and know nothing of what had happened there.

The contrast is not between the soldiers and the ignorant civilians back home, but between the survivors of earlier battles and those who came after them.

GLOSSARY

Beaucourt, Pottage, Hamel villages in eastern France where much fighting took place

The Boche French soldiers' nickname for the Germans, also used by British soldiers

a creeping minute-hand the poet remembers the last moments before the order to attack

went over went over the top of the trench to advance towards the enemy. At this point they presented a clear target to the enemy

RUDYARD KIPLING (1865–1936)

BIOGRAPHY

Born in Bombay, Kipling was educated in England at Haileybury School. He returned to India to work as a journalist. After the success of his collections of poems and short stories he returned to London to devote himself entirely to his literary career. He was awarded the Nobel Prize for Literature in 1907, and he refused the Poet Laureateship three times.

His only son, John, was killed in action in 1915. The boy was still under age, and was only able to join up through his father's influence.

Kipling was perhaps too easily seduced by popular slogans and lacked the perception to grasp wider issues, but he was a brilliant craftsman and worth listening to as a spokesman for the ordinary soldier with all his weaknesses and prejudices.

Those who think of him as a warmonger should read his *Epitaphs of War* (1914–18) and remember that for many years he financed the Last Post sounded on the Menin Gate at Ypres. The two poems discussed below were written during the Boer War but the sentiments are equally applicable to the World War still to come.

DIRGE OF DEAD SISTERS (1902) (M)

The last four lines are a variant on the second stanza; is this effective?

As is made clear by its subtitle, the poem is a tribute to the nurses who died in the Boer War (1899–1902). The poem records their heroism and devotion to duty in stanzas alternating questions and answers.

COMMENT

The question and answer form was much used by Kipling for dramatic effect. His skilful use of rhythm is shown in the poem, the relentless beat of the lines echoing the clatter of the wheels of the Red Cross trains. (The full text of the poem may be found in *The Works of Rudyard Kipling*, Wordsworth Editions. Ware, 1994, p. 218.)

GLOSSARY

Maxim type of automatic machine gun

flagless normally the coffin of a serving soldier was covered by the Union Jack

firing-party a round of gunfire was fired as a salute to the dead man

the Waiting Angel the recording angel at the Day of Judgement, the last day of the world

Uitvlugt, Simon's Town towns in South Africa; the latter is a naval base near the tip of Cape of Good Hope

Her that fell Mary Kingsley (1862–1900), niece of the author Charles Kingsley. She travelled widely in West Africa and left excellent accounts of her travels. She died during the Boer War nursing Boer prisoners

THE HYAENAS (M)

Do you think that Kipling himself was unsure about the justification of the Boer War?

This is another poem inspired by the Boer War, but it is equally applicable to the profiteers who grew rich during the First World War, like hyaenas feeding on the dead. The poet also directs his anger against those who abuse the dead because they had fallen in what many people saw as an unjust war. As elsewhere, Kipling is not concerned here with the rights and wrongs of the war, but with the fate of ordinary soldiers who died fighting the war.

COMMENT

Written in the form of a parable (see Literary Terms), the poem describes the hasty burial of a British soldier. The hyaenas soon dig up the corpse to feed on it, but at least they do not abuse the dead man's good name.

GLOSSARY

snout push with their snouts
tushes tusks, teeth

CHARLOTTE MEW (1869–1928)

BIOGRAPHY

Born in Bloomsbury, London, into a comfortable middle-class family, Charlotte Mew was educated locally. After her architect father's early death the family found itself in considerable financial difficulties. Charlotte had some success with her short stories and articles, and later began to write poetry. Oppressed by ill-health, she had no confidence in her own ability – in spite of being awarded a Civil List pension (granted by royal favour). When her beloved sister died in 1928 Charlotte Mew took her own life.

THE CENOTAPH (SEPTEMBER 1919) (C/R)

Compare Charlotte Mew's lament for the dead with Ivor Gurney's To His Love.

This poem sums up the sombre mood of many people after the war. Far from being a land fit for heroes, England had little to offer the returning soldiers. Not much had changed: sordid money-making mocked the vain sacrifice of so many young lives which are here mourned.

COMMENT

The poem opens on a note of grief for the young dead and for those left behind to mourn them. A cenotaph should be built for the dead: let the mourners cover it with flowers.

In the last nine lines the tone changes to one of stern indignation at the mockery of the sacrifice of so many just so that greed and dishonesty can flourish.

The poem raises an interesting question: when did a war started for political aims, to defeat an aggressor, come to be seen as a crusade for a better post-war England?

GLOSSARY

the wild sweet blood the adjectives stress the intoxicating quality of youth

Victory, winged the famous statue of Nike, the winged Greek goddess of victory. Discovered in Samothrace, the statue is now in the Louvre

God is not mocked see the Bible, Galatians 6:7: 'Be not deceived; God is not mocked: for whatsoever a man soweth, that shall he also reap'

ROBERT NICHOLS (1893–1944)

BIOGRAPHY

Robert Nichols fought in France until he was invalided out, shell-shocked, after the battle of the Somme (1916). He was a friend of Graves and Sassoon, through whom he also met Wilfred Owen. After the war Nichols went to the University of Tokyo as Professor of English Literature. He wrote poetry and plays occasionally, but with no great success.

COMRADES: AN EPISODE (G/M)

What is your interpretation of the words 'Why for me'?

A young officer's careless movement of the hand draws enemy fire on him. Badly wounded, he lies by the barbed wire, and all attempts to bring him back into the trench fail. As the sun rises he thinks of his men and drags himself back towards the trench. Two of his men are killed trying to rescue him. He is angry at the waste of their lives since he is dying anyway. He dies smiling at the men under his command.

COMMENT

The subtitle stresses the commonplace nature of the event described – just another man killed. The sad story is told in pairs of rhyming lines separated by a short line, which gives a disjointed effect, like the men's whispered conversation in the trench.

The officer's love for his men is worth considering, if only for its asexual nature (see the section on Love and Friendship under Themes, p. 57).

GLOSSARY

Verey a coloured signalling flare fired from a pistol
Stand to! wait for orders
Maxims automatic machine guns
No-Man's Land strip of unoccupied land separating the opposing trenches

WILFRED OWEN (1883–1918)

BIOGRAPHY

Wilfred Owen was born in Oswestry, Shropshire, the son of a railway worker and his ambitious, disappointed wife. He was educated at the Birkenhead Institute, at Shrewsbury Technical School and at the University of London. He enlisted in 1915, was commissioned in the Manchester Regiment and sent over to France later in the same year. Wounded three times, he was diagnosed as shell-shocked ('neurasthenia' was the euphemism (see Literary Terms) for this condition) in 1917 and sent to the Craiglockhart War Hospital in Edinburgh.

His time there was important to him both as a poet and as a man. He met Siegfried Sassoon (sent to the Hospital to silence his opposition to the war), Robert Graves and Robert Nichols. Sassoon's pacifism reinforced Owen's own feelings about the war. Sassoon influenced Owen's poetic style as well, encouraging him to express himself in more colloquial language.

Through Sassoon, Owen also met several prominent

literary figures in London, and it was a matter of pride to him to be treated as their equal.

Sent to Scarborough as camp commandant of officers' quarters, he had more leisure to write and particularly to work on his innovative verse technique. His use of assonance and half-rhyme (see Literary Terms) was approved of by both Graves and Charles Scott-Moncrieff (the future translator of Marcel Proust's *Remembrance of Things Past*), who had also served on the Western Front, winning the Military Cross.

In September 1918 Owen was posted back to his old battalion, and in October he was awarded the Military Cross for gallantry. A week before the war ended he was killed while leading his men across the river Sambre.

At the time of his death he was preparing his verse for publication, and his *Poems*, with Siegfried Sassoon's introduction, was published in 1920. By then Owen was acknowledged as the foremost poet of the war.

EXPOSURE (O/C)

Do you see the technical imperfections of the verse as deliberate or as the result of carelessness or haste?

The men in the trenches are awake throughout a snowy winter night, fearing an attack. Cold and miserable, they wait numbly for something to happen. They half-dream of home, and return to the cold reality, accepting their presence there as a duty in defence of what they hold dear. By the next evening many of them will be dead, lying on the frozen ground for the burying party to pick them up.

COMMENT

The form of the poem is worth noticing: the half-rhymes (silent … salient, brambles … rumbles) are disturbing because we are accustomed to perfect rhyme and expect it.

A similar disconcerting effect is achieved by the

irregular variations in the wording of the last line of each stanza. Like the soldiers in the poem we are alert, waiting for something (in our case a rhyme or an exact repetition).

GLOSSARY

salient strengthened line of defence
glozed glazed, glittering

PARABLE OF THE OLD MEN AND THE YOUNG

(This poem can be found in *Complete Poems of Wilfred Owen*, J. Stallworthy (Ed.), Chatto, Oxford, 1983.)

A comparison of the poem with the biblical story will bring out the message of the poem.

The biblical story of Abraham dutifully offering his son Isaac as a sacrifice to God (Genesis 22) is given a bitter new twist here. As in the Bible, an angel calls out to Abraham to hold his hand. Having proved his readiness to obey God's command and kill his son he is released from carrying out the command. In Owen's poem, however, the old man (i.e. the military Establishment) in his pride kills his son nevertheless, along with half the young men of Europe.

COMMENT

The mock-biblical language (clave, spake, builded) stresses the harsh mockery of the authorities who, in their arrogance, go on with the slaughter, killing whole generations of young men. The pacific message is quite clear.

GLOSSARY

burnt-offering anything burnt on the altar as a sacrificial offering to the gods
seed children

THE SEND-OFF (P/O)

Pick out the words and phrases that create the furtive atmosphere.

The poem describes a night scene at a railway siding where troops are starting out on their journey to France. They marched in, singing, their tunics decorated with flowers given to them by cheering girls, but once they are inside their train it goes off in silence, furtively. How many of them will return? And will they come back in triumph, or will they creep silently back to their villages?

COMMENT

The poem attacks the facile patriotism of the civilians and implies that there is a certain shamefulness about the whole proceedings, a guilty conspiracy of silence, symbolised by the winking lamp.

The form of the poem is interesting. It consists of iambic pentameters (see Literary Terms), alternating with metrically irregular half-lines achieving the stuttering effect of a train in motion.

GLOSSARY

As men's are, dead like the floral tributes at a funeral
not ours not from our regiment
what women meant the women's shallow patriotism

DULCE ET DECORUM EST (M/C/P/O)

Read Jessie Pope's Who's for the Game? *to understand Owen's anger.*

The men are marching back to their post, dead tired and oblivious to the enemy gas shells. So it happens that they are taken by surprise, and one man, too slow in putting on his gas mask, dies horribly.

The last four lines are an attack on a glib patriotic writer (identified as Jessie Pope, a journalist and author of three volumes of jolly patriotic poems).

COMMENT

The poem is a description of a gas attack and the resulting horrible death of one of the men, and the reader is spared none of the dreadful details. If people in England could witness his death – perhaps in some nightmare dream – they would not say that it is sweet to die for one's country.

GLOSSARY

Dulce et decorum est pro patria mori a quotation from the Latin poet Horace (65–8BC), *Odes,* III, iii, 13
Gas! the Germans used mustard gas which destroyed the

tissues of the lungs and caused internal bleeding. The victim in fact choked to death on his own blood

My friend it is certain that Owen was addressing Jessie Pope (an earlier version of the poem is dedicated to her)

MENTAL CASES (C/P)

Can you pick out the images of horror? What is the purpose of accumulating them?

The first stanza of this poem consists of rhetorical questions which are answered in the second and third stanzas. The grinning madmen described in the opening stanza are the inmates of a military hospital, those whose minds gave way under the horrors they had witnessed. They are doomed to go on remembering what they had seen, and if they pluck at our sleeves it is to remind us that we put them in their hell.

COMMENT

Owen offers one picture of grotesque horror after another, deliberately so, as if to punish us for our share in the responsibility for the war.

Reflecting the confusion of these men's minds, the form of the poem is irregular, with one pair of rhyming lines, irregularly placed, in each stanza. The tension is heightened by the use of ellipsis ('Who these hellish?') and stilted syntax (see Literary Terms).

GLOSSARY

fretted marked with veins

Rucked piled up

rope-knouts knotted whips (there may be an oblique reference to the scourging of Christ here)

FUTILITY (M/C/P/O)

A dead soldier has been placed in the sun. A countryman, he had been an early riser, and perhaps the sun will wake him again once more. It warms seeds into life, and once, a long time ago, it brought life to the dead planet Earth. If it cannot wake the soldier now, why was he ever given life, why was the Earth ever awakened at all?

COMMENT

When reading Owen's poetry you are constantly reminded of the hard work he put in on the form of his verse.

This is a quiet, sad poem, as if spoken by men whispering round the corpse, trying to revive it. The mood, however, is not one of quiet resignation but of indignation: if a man can be killed for nothing, why give him life in the first place?

Notice the half-rhymes (once … France, star …stir, see Literary Terms), less striking here than in some of Owen's other poems, and so in keeping with the subdued tone of the poem.

GLOSSARY

whispering of fields unsown reminding him of the work to be done

the clays of a cold star the Earth

clay man, made by God out of the dust of the ground (see the Bible, Genesis 2:7)

DISABLED (M/C/P)

The subject of this poem is a young soldier, legless and armless as the result of his terrible injuries. Though still under age, he had volunteered for one of the Scottish regiments, because it seemed the right thing to do.

The restrained tone of the poem contrasts with its tragic content. Consider how effective this is.

He had been a great athlete, popular with the girls. Now he sits in his wheelchair, listening to boys playing football in the park and watching the girls as they avert their eyes from him. He only wishes the nurses would wheel him back to bed.

COMMENT

The poem plays on our feelings with ironical cross-references: the boys in the park going home to bed ('mothered'), and the soldier's fretful wish that closes the poem ('Why don't they come/And put him into bed?').

The spurting blood of his wounds is set against the trickle of blood on his thigh when he was carried shoulder-high by his mates after a victorious football match. The crowd's welcome of the returning soldiers is in sharp contrast to the roar of the football crowd.

The unthinking simplicity of the boy is reflected in the plain, simple language. The effect is all the more telling when we piece together his disjointed thoughts and imagine the empty years stretching ahead of him.

There is no need to spell out the theme of the poem: 'the pity of War'. This phrase of Owen's which appears in the draft of the Preface to his poems, embraces pity for the dead and wounded, sorrow for the waste, helpless regret for the whole wretched business of war.

GLOSSARY

ghastly suit of grey hospital pyjamas
silly for his face eagear to paint him
lost his colour lost a lot of blood
daggers in plaid socks skean-dhu, the ornamental dagger, is inserted into the knee-sock as part of full Highland dress
Esprit de corps (*French*) loyalty to the regiment

ANTHEM FOR DOOMED YOUTH (M/P/O)

What method is used by Owen to contrast the battlefield with an English village?

This is one of Owen's best-known poems, and one that repays close study. Its plan is simple. With bitter irony, the first stanza translates the pandemonium of battle into funeral rites for the fallen, and the second stanza continues the metaphor (see Literary Terms) in the quiet of a stricken English village.

COMMENT

The stanzas are irregular in length, and half-rhymes (see Literary Terms) as well as perfect rhymes are used. Onomatopoeia (see Literary Terms) is used to suggest the sounds of gunfire.

In the first stanza Owen uses aural images only (the booming guns, the rattle of rifle fire, the moaning of the shells). In contrast the second stanza uses visual images only, as if to stress the silence of the mourning

English village: tearful eyes glittering like candles, girls' pale faces serving as a funereal pall, dusk falling like blinds being drawn in a house of mourning.

GLOSSARY

passing-bells bells rung to announce a death

pall cloth covering for a coffin

SPRING OFFENSIVE (P)

Owen seems reluctant to speak of death by name. Identify his metaphors for it.

The soldiers are waiting for the order to attack. It is a warm spring day, and some of the men are asleep, while others stand watching the horizon and wondering if they will survive the day.

When at last the order comes through, they race over the brow of the hill. They are of course exposed to enemy fire, and many of them are killed. The few who return, having done their share of killing, are silent, reluctant to speak of the fallen.

COMMENT

Though Owen took a lot of trouble over this poem (as his manuscript corrections show), his concern did not extend to the rhyme scheme which varies throughout (unlike, say, Blunden, Owen hardly ever maintains a formal rhyme pattern).

GLOSSARY

Chasmed dropped sharply

drave (*archaic*) drove

THE SENTRY (C/P)

The action is concentrated in the middle one of three stanzas. Think about the function of the other two stanzas.

The men are sheltering from heavy enemy bombardment in an old German dugout. A shell hits their sentry who survives but is blinded. In the madness of the enemy onslaught the man is heard shrieking that he can see his comrades' lights at last (a symptom of returning eyesight). Their lights had gone out long ago: he is blind.

COMMENT

As in his *Dulce Et Decorum Est,* Owen starts with a matter-of-fact narrative before plunging into a catalogue of horrors. The disjointed sentences of the last stanza convey the speaker's distress at what he had witnessed.

GLOSSARY

Boche French army slang for a German, used by British soldiers as well

whizz-bangs light shells which fly at more than speed of sound

STRANGE MEETING (C/P/O)

The speaker is a soldier who had escaped from the battle into a tunnel full of sleeping men. One of them starts up and stares at him with a smile of recognition. The soldier suddenly realises that they are all in hell, dead, but safe from the battle.

The two men lament the waste of their lives, thrown away in a war that will go on and on. The other man had recognised in the speaker the enemy soldier who had killed him the day before. They were enemies then, but now it is time to sleep.

COMMENT

Compare the use of the sound of the words with the visual images.

This is perhaps Owen's greatest poem, and certainly his best-known one. He took great pains over it, and we are fortunate to have his manuscript version, with his corrections. (It can be found, for instance, in *The Penguin Book of First World War Poetry*, edited by J. Silkin, or in the Blunden edition of Owen's *Poems*, Chatto, London, 1946.)

Critics have pointed out the literary sources of this poem (Dante's *Inferno*, Shelley's R*evolt of Islam*, Canto V, xiii, 'Laon and Cythna'). Yet these literary parallels in the setting of the poem, though interesting, are not relevant to its meaning.

The power of the poem lies first of all in the great

image of the tunnel filled with sleeping men. Legends of sleeping warriors waiting to be called are to be found in many cultures: the British legend of King Arthur and his knights is one.

The man who faces the speaker, his enemy, is also his reflection in the mirror, a *Doppelgänger* (a double), another powerful image. Here it is used in a new way: the man and his reflection are both equally the victims of the war, sharing the same ideals and emotions. The *Doppelgänger* theme is therefore used to stress the common humanity of two men from opposing armies, to reinforce the message that in killing your enemy you are killing yourself.

The poem may be unfinished (there is some doubt about this), but the abrupt ending could not be bettered for dramatic effect. The use of half-rhymes or imperfect rhymes (groined … groaned, moan … mourn, see Literary Terms) has a dramatic function as well, imitating the dim echoing of voices in the vast tunnel. It has also been suggested that the absence of the expected perfect rhyme causes us to feel uneasy and thus makes us more receptive to the atmosphere of the poem.

GLOSSARY

titanic wars in Greek mythology the wars between the Titans, and Zeus and the Olympians. The phrase emphasises the huge scale of the war

groined vaulted

cess tax, i.e. the extortionate demands of war. (There may be a hint here at 'cesspool', a pool in which water – or blood – collects)

TEST YOURSELF

Identify the speaker.

Identify the person 'to whom' this comment refers.

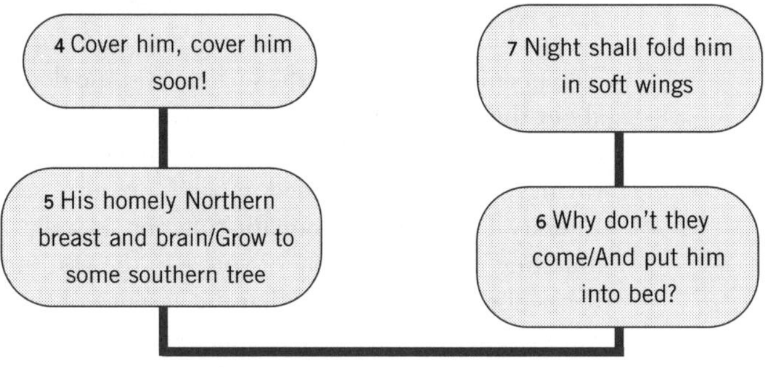

Check your answers on page 73.

B *Consider these issues.*

a What we find in Brooke's and Grenfell's poems that makes them typical of the early period of the war.

b Whether there is a place for Hardy's *In Time of 'The Breaking of Nations'* among the war poems of the First World War.

c What similarities and differences there are between Grenfell's *Into Battle* and Owen's *Spring Offensive* that are separated by about three years.

d What you remember best about Owen's poems, e.g. his descriptions of the battlefront, or his emotions of anger and pity at what he sees.

e What the following differences of approach tell you about the authors' experience of the war: Charlotte Mew's anger in *The Cenotaph* which is directed against the profiteers, compared to Owen's rage against the warmongers wasting human lives.

Jessie Pope (1868–1941)

Biography

Imagine a conversation between Jessie Pope and the disabled soldier of Owen's poem.

Jessie Pope was born in Leicester and educated at the North London Collegiate School. A working journalist, she wrote articles and fiction for various popular magazines and newspapers, including *Punch*. During the war she published three volumes of verse, *War Poems* (1915), *More War Poems* (1916) and *Simple Rhymes for Stirring Times* (1916), the last of which contains the poem discussed below. All three are characterised by a hearty, often offensive, patriotism. The last four lines of Owen's *Dulce Et Decorum Est* are addressed to her.

Who's for the game? (M)

A piece of crude war propaganda, it was published at the start of the great battles of 1916 which were to cost so many lives and turn so many people against the war. It is hard now to accept a patriotic mood that could express its recruiting enthusiasm in the words 'who would much rather come back with a crutch'.

Comment

A comparison of this poem with Owen's *Dulce Et Decorum Est* is inevitable, but we might also compare it with another Owen poem, *Disabled.* Pope's tasteless equation of war with a game of rugby should be read alongside the thoughts of the maimed ex-footballer.

Glossary

the show a popular slang word for the war

Isaac Rosenberg (1890–1918)

Biography

Isaac Rosenberg's parents were Jewish immigrants from Lithuania, desperately poor and always dependent on Jewish charities. He was educated at the local East End board school (in London) where his gifts for writing and drawing attracted his teachers' attention. After he left school friends helped him to go to the Slade School of Art. While still at the Slade he exhibited his paintings at the Whitechapel Art Gallery, and published a volume of poetry called *Night and Day*.

He was encouraged in his writing by Rupert Brooke's friend and admirer Edward Marsh (1872–1953) though it is doubtful whether Marsh's influence was wholly beneficial. He was baffled by Rosenberg's verse, and tried to direct him towards a more conventional style – fortunately without success.

Soon after war was declared Rosenberg enlisted, not for any patriotic reasons (he was a pacifist) but so that his mother would receive a separation allowance.

Early in 1916 he was sent to France and though unfit for war service in every way (he was small, sickly, clumsy and hopelessly absent-minded) he survived until 1918, and was killed in action on 1 April, April Fools' Day - a date that seems to underline the stupid waste of his life.

Rosenberg is regarded by many as second only to Owen as a poet of the war. They were utter opposites: while Owen was racked by anger and guilt, Rosenberg remained largely detached, recording the horrors round him with a painter's eye.

BREAK OF DAY IN THE TRENCHES (C/P/O)

The poet is watching a cheerful rat outside the trench, and thinking that the creature is equally at home in British and German trenches, and seems to find the madness of the war amusing. The poppies round the trench, grown out of men's spilled blood, are dropping one by one in the turmoil of battle, but the poppy which the poet had cheerfully stuck behind his ear seems safe enough.

COMMENT

There are touches of humour in the first half of the poem: the rat's antics, the poet's jaunty poppy. The

Which emotions can you identify in Rosenberg's poem?

mood changes as the poet begins to think about the war. The poppies round the trench grow where men had fallen, and the flowers too will fall as the shells explode.

The poppy had a special significance for the soldiers on the Western Front who believed that the flower owed its brilliant colour to all the spilt blood that had soaked into the soil. In December 1915 *Punch* published a poem, *In Flanders Fields*, by a Canadian medical officer, John McCrae (1872–1918). The poem honours the sacrifice of the fallen of whom the poppy became a symbol.

GLOSSARY

druid Time sunrise when the ancient druidic ceremonies used to take place

Less chanced having less of a lucky chance

DEAD MAN'S DUMP (C/P/O)

The poem describes the hellish landscape of the war. Carts loaded with the wounded drive over the unburied dead. As the wounded men die their bodies join those of men killed earlier. One man dies just as the cart reaches him, and the wheels go over his face.

COMMENT

Compare this poem to Owen's The Sentry, *identifying the similarities and differences.*

One of the best poems to come out of the war, it is perhaps also the most shattering, and lives up to its ugly title. The tortured images match the painful subject matter. Rosenberg seems to wrestle with the language to find expression for the unutterable horrors he has seen.

Yet his concern in this mad hell of destruction is for the fate of the soul, and he follows each death with wonder.

The last two stanzas tell of a dying man who longs for the cart to come. It arrives just too late, and its wheels go over his dead face. What the poet has to tell is dreadful, yet the lines are filled with pity.

GLOSSARY

limbers detachable front parts of gun carriages which can be used as carts

soul's sack dead body

God-ancestralled God-given

ichor in classical mythology the divine liquid flowing through the gods' veins

SIEGFRIED SASSOON (1886–1967)

BIOGRAPHY

Born in Kent into a wealthy aristocratic family, Sassoon was educated at Marlborough College and Clare College, Cambridge. He left without taking a degree to devote himself to his twin passions, fox-hunting and cricket.

Just before the outbreak of the war he enlisted as a cavalry soldier and in 1915 was commissioned in the Royal Welch Fusiliers.

In 1916 he was awarded the Military Cross for bravery. In April 1917 he was wounded and sent to a hospital in England. Increasingly troubled by the senseless continuation of the war, Sassoon sent an anti-war statement to his commanding officer, which was read out in the House of Commons and reprinted in full in *The Times*. With Graves as his witness before the medical board, Sassoon was declared shell-shocked and sent to the Craiglockhart War Hospital in Edinburgh – a convenient way of silencing his protest. At Craiglockhart he met Wilfred Owen to whom he gave much encouragement.

He was sent back to France and in July 1918 he was wounded again and eventually retired from the army. By this time he was the leading war poet and hero of the anti-war faction. He became Literary Editor of the *Daily Herald*, published his *War Poems* (1928) and his fictional three-volume autobiography (*The Memoirs of a Fox-Hunting Man*, *The Memoirs of an Infantry Officer* and *Sherston's Progress*, 1929–36). His literary reputation rests on this autobiography as much as on his poems.

THE GENERAL (M/C/O)

The General cheerfully inspects the troops, who like his friendliness. All the same, most of them are going to die thanks to both his incompetence and the incompetence of his staff.

COMMENT

Could this short poem be written in conventional poetic language and still be effective?

The poem is all the more effective for its anecdotal form, especially for the biting payoff in the last line.

The language is colloquial and there is not a trace of heroism. The hate for the incompetent guilty men at the top of the military command is typical of Sassoon's later work.

GLOSSARY

the line the line of battle

Arras town in northern France, the scene of a 1917 battle with huge casualties

BASE DETAILS (M/C/P)

See how Sassoon establishes the Major's social status and in doing so mocks him.

The poem is short, the language colloquial, the rhyme scheme neat. It is an attack on the officers at the base, comfortably eating and drinking, well out of the line of fire. They have a word or two of pity for the fallen, but they do not really care at all, and will die in their beds back home in England after the war.

COMMENT

While *The General* attacks the stupidity of the General Staff, *Base Details* turns on their uncaring attitude, their arrogance. (It is now generally accepted that the large number of casualties could have been avoided, had it been considered important to save lives.)

GLOSSARY

Base Details the title is a pun on 'base' which can also mean 'dishonourable'

Roll of Honour casualty list

scrap battle

DOES IT MATTER? (M/P)

Compare this poem to Owen's Disabled. *Sassoon is too angry to spare time for pity.*

A savage attack on the glib words of comfort offered to the mutilated victims of the war. If you have lost your legs, people will be kind as long as you keep a stiff upper lip and do not talk about it. If you have been blinded, you will be taught handicraft work, and if you drink to forget the horrors, people will be tolerant.

COMMENT

The poem is shot through with bitter irony at the treatment of 'war heroes'.

The reader's attention is drawn more to the hypocritical comforters than to the maimed men.

GLOSSARY

muffins and eggs the traditional dish at the lavish hunting teas. Sassoon, the 'fox-hunting man', knew all about them

sit on the terrace i.e. in a veterans' home

the pit hell

SUICIDE IN THE TRENCHES (M/C)

Both Owen and Sassoon attack the ignorance and hypocrisy of the home front. Compare their methods.

The poet remembers a young soldier, cheerful, not very bright, happy in his simple way. The misery of the winter trenches undid him, and he shot himself. No-one ever spoke of him again. Those who cheer the marching soldiers on their way to the front should thank God for their ignorance of the hell of the trenches.

COMMENT

The simple, jaunty rhythm camouflages the bitterness of Sassoon's poem.

His feelings break through in the last stanza which contrasts the smug people at home with the reality of the war.

GLOSSARY

soldier boy, soldier lads a mockery of the jolly phrases employed by the British popular press

crumps explosions of heavy bombs

THE HERO (M/C)

An officer is paying a visit of condolence to the mother of one of his fellow officers. He does not tell her the truth – that her son was a coward who put his comrades at risk and was killed while trying to get himself sent back home. Instead, the officer tells her lies about her son's bravery in order to comfort her.

Do you think the lies are justified? Does Sassoon?

COMMENT

The full irony of the title and of the first line is revealed in the second and third stanzas, with contempt for the coward running through the third stanza.

There is compassion for the dead man's mother tempered perhaps by the officer's (and Sassoon's) dislike of her proud patriotic phrases. Again the gulf between the soldiers and the civilians is made clear.

It is interesting that Sassoon while hating the war passionately, still had nothing but contempt for a coward.

GLOSSARY

Brother Officer the courtesy title for a fellow officer adds here a note of irony

cold-footed cowardly

Wicked corner the soldiers' nickname for a dangerous section of the trenches

ATROCITIES (K)

A hatred of cowardice and cruelty pervades the poem, and finds expression in bitter irony, addressing the man

Spot the differences between this coward and Sassoon's 'Hero'.

who cleverly pretended to be sick when the situation looked dangerous, and lied his way home. The coward had enough courage to kill defenceless prisoners, lobbing grenades into their dugout.

COMMENT

As has been noted above, Sassoon hated the war, yet he also hated those who tried to escape from it, by dishonest means.

GLOSSARY

Camerad! the German soldiers used the word *Kamerad* (friend) when surrendering

CHARLES HAMILTON SORLEY (1895–1915)

BIOGRAPHY

Educated at Marlborough College, Charles Hamilton Sorley won a scholarship to University College, Oxford, but went first to Germany for six months and was nearly trapped there by the outbreak of the war. Instead of going up to Oxford he enlisted, was commissioned in the Sussex Regiment and sent to France in May 1915. He was killed in October of the same year in the Battle of Loos. His book of poetry, *Marlborough and Other Poems*, was published posthumously and reprinted several times. His poetic voice and the maturity of his judgement are unusual for one so young.

ALL THE HILLS AND VALES ALONG (C/P/O)

This extraordinary poem begins as an enthusiastic marching song but the enthusiasm is soon tempered by irony. Small men live, great men die, therefore we must welcome death. The indifferent earth will receive us, echoing the tramp of our marching feet long after we are dead.

COMMENT

The first discordant note is the use of the colloquial 'chaps', out of place in the rhetoric of a patriotic poem.

Compare Sorley's attitude to death in battle with Grenfell's.

The men should die without regret, for far greater men had died before them. The earth will receive them happily as she had greeted the death of both Socrates and Christ.

The last four lines resolve any doubt about the meaning of the poem, as the ironical note sounds ever clearer: you might as well die merrily for die you must.

GLOSSARY

Barabbas the condemned thief who was chosen by the Jews to be released instead of Christ who was crucified (see the Bible, Matthew 27:15–23)

Socrates Athenian philosopher (469–399BC) condemned to death on the charge of introducing new gods and corrupting the young. He was given a cup of hemlock to drink, a common way of carrying out the death sentence in ancient Athens

EDWARD THOMAS (1878–1917)

BIOGRAPHY

Edward Thomas was educated at St Paul's School in London and at Lincoln College, Oxford. He married while still an undergraduate, and while his wife Helen proved an invaluable companion and later a proud guardian of his work, his early marriage meant that he was always beset by financial anxieties. He made a living by writing articles, descriptive pieces and biographies, many of them simply potboilers.

He was encouraged by the American poet Robert Frost to write poetry, but constant money problems hindered his work. He enlisted in 1915 and was commissioned in the Royal Garrison Artillery. Once he was on officer's pay, he was free of financial anxieties for the first time in his life and could devote his free time to writing poetry. He was sent to France in March 1917 and was killed at Arras a month later.

His poems on the English countryside have great

beauty, and his war poems (of which there are only a few, as he preferred to cling to his memories of England as a way of preserving his sanity) are justly valued. His innate melancholy accords well with themes of war and death.

AS THE TEAM'S HEAD-BRASS (C/P/O)

Notice how the war theme is introduced and gradually developed.

The poet sits on a fallen tree at the edge of a field, watching a ploughman with his team of horses at work. A pair of lovers pass on their way to the wood to make love. Each time the team passes the poet, he and the ploughman talk a little, mostly about the war. The ploughman's mate was killed in France, and if he were alive still, they would have shifted the fallen tree together. If there had been no war, everything would have been different.

COMMENT

The war is a silent presence, all the more powerful and threatening for the peace of this corner of the field. Against the background of the war, Thomas presents an English landscape of enduring modest beauty that speaks for peace, for life. By implication this is a deeply poignant piece of work, as well as a poem of great beauty.

There is a curious parallel between the plan of this poem and that of Hardy's *In Time of 'The Breaking of Nations'*.

GLOSSARY

the team's head-brass the brass ornaments on the horses' bridles

Charlock wild mustard, a yellow weed

out on active service in France

TEST YOURSELF

Identify the speaker.

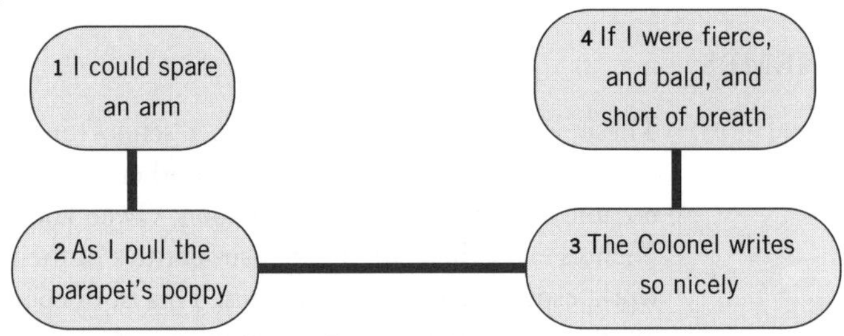

Identify the person 'to whom' this comment refers.

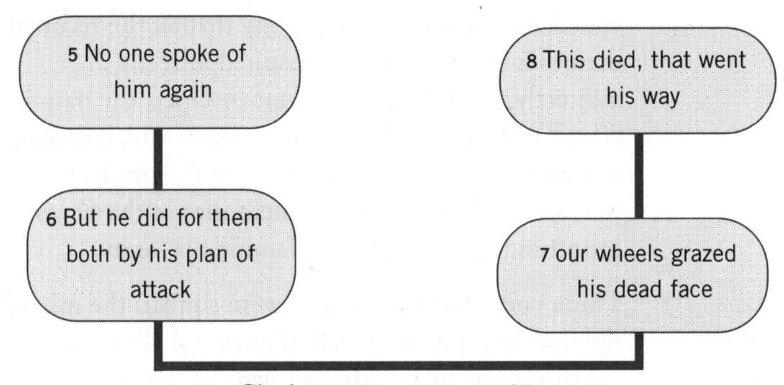

Check your answers on page 73.

B *Consider these issues.*

a If you selected a few poems spanning the war years, and tried to trace the change of mood in the army, which poems you would choose and what would bring about the change.

b Sassoon's views of the General Staff and where he expresses them.

c If Sassoon and Owen agree in their views of the civilians at home.

d If you wrote out a plan of Sorley's *All the Hills and Vales Along*, how you would show the sequence of his thoughts.

e What makes *As the Team's Head-Brass* a war poem.

COMMENTARY

THEMES

These poets certainly did not form a 'school': indeed not many of them even knew one another – with the notable exception of Graves, Sassoon, Owen and Nichols – yet there are marked similarities in their work, especially regarding themes. This is, of course, hardly surprising since these young men shared a shattering experience which shaped, and in many cases ended, their lives. You might say that all the recurring themes in their work were inspired, directly or indirectly, by the war. Thus, for instance, the nature poems of Edward Thomas, even those which contain few direct references to the war, are the product of the war, since Thomas used his memories of the English countryside as a means of retaining his sanity.

The similarity of war experiences is reflected in the similarity of themes.

These poets' war experiences were similar: the misery of the trenches, the noisy hell of enemy shelling, the casualties, the many different ways of dying.

Their reactions to these events were similar too. Most of them were young officers, acutely aware of their responsibility for their men, and of the irresponsibility of the General Staff. Affection and pity for the soldiers, and anger and bitterness against the authorities and against the posturing patriots at home are heard very clearly in many of the poems.

Not surprisingly, the nature of the poetry changed as the war went on. Once the great battles of 1916 (Verdun, Somme) had taken place, there was no call for patriotic poems like Rupert Brooke's (especially his *Peace*) or marching songs like Grenfell's, nor even for C.H. Sorley's dissenting voice.

Perhaps it was the depth of the shared experience of horrors that strengthened the affection in which these men held one another, and the anguished responsibility of the young officers for their men. Certainly the verse grows more personal. It is based on individual experiences and takes for its subject not the faceless marching column, but individuals, men whom the reader will remember ('old Stevens' in Blunden's *The Zonnebeke Road*, the Buckinghamshire chatterer in Gurney's *The Silent One* (C/P/O), the country boy who killed himself in Sassoon's *Suicide in the Trenches*). What comes across very clearly is the officers' concern for their men as people.

THE WOUNDED AND THE DEAD

The one theme that stands out is, of course, death, and the many cruel ways of dying this war had invented.

There is a world of difference between death imagined by Rupert Brooke in *The Dead* (C/P) as a 'shining peace' and in *Peace* as 'the laughing heart's long peace', and the man choking on gas in Owen's *Dulce Et Decorum Est* or the blinded sentry shrieking through broken teeth in his *The Sentry*.

There is no forgetting for these poets. Their world has

changed forever, and the images of horror will stay with them through their lives. Wilfred Owen's poetry conveys very convincingly the persistence of nightmare memories. If writers like Robert Graves (*A Dead Boche* (M), *The Two Fusiliers*) and Siegfried Sassoon (*Atrocities*, *The Hero* or *Died of Wounds* (G/M)) succeed in retaining a measure of detachment and of freedom from self-reproach, is this simply due to the habit of self-control, of the 'stiff upper lip' that Sassoon mocks in *Does It Matter?*

Anger at the horror of war

All these poets also share their anger at what had been allowed to happen. Their anger is directed against the military leadership and also against the glib patriotism of the people back home. Sassoon uses sarcasm with good effect in *Base Details* and *The General* while Owen conveys his controlled anger in *Disabled*, *Anthem for Doomed Youth* and *Dulce Et Decorum Est*, as well as his deep pity, 'The eternal reciprocity of tears' (*Insensibility* (C/O/P)), in *Mental Cases* and *Disabled.* He is, of course, the author of, for many, the greatest war poem on death, *Strange Meeting*. As if distanced by the depth of the vaulted tunnel his anger and pity have a stately calm, purged by pain. Sassoon's anger in *Blighters* (C) is also unmistakable.

THE HOME FRONT

Note the soldiers' dislike of glib patriotism.

We have spoken of the anger felt by the men on the Western Front – not only at the reckless incompetence of the leadership but also at the hypocrisy and wilful blindness of the British public, who, for a very long time, succeeded in ignoring the horrible reality of the war.

It is Owen again who speaks out in *Dulce Et Decorum Est* (quite specifically in an earlier version) against jingoistic writers like Jessie Pope who, from the safety of their homes, urged the soldiers to sacrifice their lives in fighting the 'beastly Germans'.

Although the fraternisation by opposing armies at Rouges Bancs in France on Christmas Day 1914 was never to be repeated, by and large, most soldiers came to dislike the enemy rather less and the loud-mouthed patriots at home rather more. As Edward Thomas puts it in *This is No Case of Petty Right or Wrong* (P): 'Beside my hate for one fat patriot/My hatred of the Kaiser is love true'.

This way of thinking remained for a long time incomprehensible to the people at home who could not see why the soldiers seemed so lukewarm in sharing their patriotic sentiments. There was a growing gulf between the fighting men and the cheering women at home; Owen's *The Send-Off* and Sassoon's *Glory of Women* (C/P/O) make this quite clear, as does a clever little poem entitled *Subalterns* (R/O) by Elizabeth Daryush, daughter of the Poet Laureate Robert Bridges. While the young woman gushes in high-flown phrases, the young officer stutters in embarrassment.

Not all women, of course, persisted in their wilful ignorance. There were many who were aware of what Vera Brittain in her *Testament of Youth* called 'that terrible barrier of knowledge by which War cut off the men who possessed it from the women who remained in ignorance'.

The women at home: their guilt and frustration

Inevitably these women experienced a feeling of guilt for not sharing the dangers, and perhaps also some resentment at being prevented in playing a part in the war. It is neatly expressed in a sad poem by Gabrielle Elliot, *Pierrot Goes to War* (R): 'Pierrot goes forward – but what of Pierrette?'

This feeling of frustration was all the stronger among young women as the position of women in Britain was changing, largely because of the war. Increasingly employed away from the house, mostly on war work, even if only indirectly, women were gaining economic independence, and with it a measure of self-confidence which expressed itself more and more strongly in the demand for voting rights for women.

The suffragette movement certainly existed before the war, but without the war it would have had to struggle much longer and much harder to achieve its aims. Certainly the suffragettes had fought their battles (often literally, in the streets, outside Parliament) before the war, but the role of women in the wartime national economy, especially in the munition factories, was a powerful argument for women's political rights. (Women in Britain gained limited rights to vote in 1918 and full voting rights in 1928.)

As more and more women chose to work in factories rather than in domestic service, the pampered middle- and upper-class women found themselves a little less pampered in a changing world.

For the soldiers in the trenches, dreaming of the home fires burning, the idea of their wives going out to work contributed to their growing sense of alienation from the people back in Britain. As has already been noted, the main cause of this was their inability, or unwillingness, to make anyone at home comprehend the full horror of trench warfare. The British public was encouraged in its ignorance by the popular British press which already possessed enormous power of persuasion and used it unscrupulously.

Yet if the press reports were often misleading, the appalling carnage was clear from the casualty lists. (After the Somme (1916) only officers' casualty lists were published.) As a whole generation of young men was pretty well wiped out, a whole generation of young women was condemned to spinsterhood.

The suffering of these young women, however real and deep, did not inspire any great poetry, as a glance through any anthology of women's verse of the period will show. It was left to poets like Wilfred Owen and Edward Thomas to give expression to the grief of the 'sad shires' (as Owen puts it in *Anthem for Doomed Youth*).

LOVE AND FRIENDSHIP

Homosexuality In recent years much has been written about the homosexual element in the poetry of the First World War. It is possible that Gurney and Sassoon, and perhaps Owen too, had homosexual leanings. As Graves remarks in his autobiography *Goodbye to All That*, in English public schools romance was necessarily homosexual (though most boys reverted to heterosexuality as they grew older), and most of the war poets were public schoolboys. Yet to explain the emotion that bound these men together in purely sexual terms is a naïve oversimplification.

The experiences which these men had undergone had obviously forged strong ties, the 'wet bonds of blood' that held Graves's *Two Fusiliers*. (Owen's *Apologia Pro Poemate Meo* (P) contains a clear reference to this love: 'fellowships –/Untold of happy lovers in old song'.)

There were other ties apart from the fellowship of dangers shared: there was the loyalty of the men to their officers, and the officers' sense of responsibility for their men. It is touching to think of these officers, some of them barely in their twenties, taking care of their men, trying to sort out their home problems, fighting alongside them and often dying with them too. The relationship between the officer and his men was often almost paternal, however young the officer was, and there was no physical element to be found there. Robert Nichols in his *Comrades: an Episode* tried to express this bond of affection between the dying officer and his men, and though he is not entirely successful in this, yet his poem does convey something of the mutual concern and affection.

The homosexual interpretation of these complex relationships finds some support in poems attacking the women back in England, but this could be missing the point. What is being attacked is the hysterical jingoism so repugnant to those who did the fighting. Admittedly, there were many young women who embraced this unattractive patriotism very eagerly. It was young women who offered white feathers (symbols of cowardice) to men in the street who were not in uniform and who were therefore judged by these young women to be cowards shirking their military duty. (Tales were told of young men offered the white feather who turned out to be convalescing war wounded!)

The anger poets like Sassoon (*Glory of Women* – C/P/O) and Owen (*Dulce Et Decorum Est*) expressed in their verse was against the prevailing hysteria and the women who participated in it (they may well have done so because women could not play an active part in the war).

NATURE

There is another major theme running through the poetry of the First World War, and that is, surprisingly perhaps, that of nature. There is the battle-scarred Flemish and French landscape described so well by Edmund Blunden and Isaac Rosenberg, and there is the green, smiling English countryside of the poets' memories.

The English landscape remembered

Some of them, notably Edward Thomas, blotted out their present nightmare completely through their recollections of England (see, for instance, his beautifully accurate description of a small corner of England in *As the Team's Head-Brass*). Ivor Gurney, too, retained his vivid memories of England, and in his poem *To His Love* we find an evocative sketch of his beloved Cotswolds where the sheep graze and 'take no heed'.

The landscape of war

By contrast, in Edward Blunden's verse the ghastly Flemish landscape, barren, shell-pitted, wound round with barbed wire, remains so vivid that even after the war, back home once again, he sees it more clearly than the southern English countryside round him ('the charred stub outspeaks the living tree', *1916 seen from 1921*).

Rosenberg, the painter, observes the landscape before him to the last detail, and describes what he sees, whether it is the cheerful rat's antics outside the trench or the earth convulsed by bombardment, ghastly with piled corpses. To him we owe that one moment of joy of the larks' song heard by the terrified men in *Returning, We Hear the Larks* (C/P/O).

Owen and Sassoon (and to a lesser extent Robert Graves), the most 'engaged' of the war poets, were too concerned with the issues of the soldiers' lives and deaths to notice the landscape much. Nevertheless, taking the poetry of the First World War as a whole and especially contrasting it with its continental counterparts (for instance the German poets Georg Trakl and August Stramm, and the Frenchmen Charles Vildrac and Guillaume Apollinaire), we cannot fail to notice that, for the English poets, landscape retained its power to command their attention and to give comfort. Perhaps it says something about the significant role of nature in English lyrical poetry.

Language & imagery

The power of the image

Images are what makes poetry – the use of verbal pictures not only to describe what the poet sees, but also, most importantly in these war poems, to express complex emotions and thoughts.

Think of a line like Owen's 'And each slow dusk a drawing-down of blinds' (*Anthem for Doomed Youth*). The words 'slow dusk' evoke the gradual approach of the evening in the English countryside, while 'a drawing-down of blinds' merges the peaceful night-time ritual of drawing the curtains with the drawing-down of blinds in a house of mourning. Thus each evening is a re-enactment of the mourning for a dead soldier that takes place in house after house.

Winter and sleep as metaphors of death

The metaphors (see Literary Terms) of winter, snow and ice representing death, recur throughout this war poetry; naturally enough if we remember the misery of winter trenches. Yet the metaphor reaches beyond descriptions of physical misery to an image of annihilation.

Edmund Blunden recalls with a shudder the landscape of Flanders, filled with symbols of death (*The Zonnebeke Road*, *Zillebeke Brook* (C)) though perhaps his most powerful image of death is to be found in a peacetime poem, *The Midnight Skaters* (P), where death is seen lurking beneath the ice, hating the skaters through the glass of ice. In all these images the metaphors are used not to soften the presentation of death, but to strengthen its impact.

Another image of death is of course sleep, most clearly presented in Owen's *Asleep* (C) with the dead man curled up as if asleep, while the blood trickles slowly from his fatal wound.

Sleep brings dreams, and for these poets they can only be nightmares (the gassed soldier in Owen's *Dulce Et Decorum Est*, the nightmare memories in Sassoon's *Repression of War Experience* (C/P), and in his *Does it Matter?*).

Death and sleep are inextricably merged, nowhere more

strikingly than in Owen's *Strange Meeting*. The whole poem may be seen as an extended metaphor of death, as a reconciliation and peace, and also as a shared acceptance of the futility and waste of war. There could be no better illustration of the potential of an image for conveying a wealth of pictures, of complex thoughts and emotions.

The Flanders poppy

There is one metaphor that entered the poetry of the war through the imagination of the soldiers in the trenches. They came to believe that the Flanders poppy owed its brilliant colour to the blood that had soaked into the soil. Largely through the medium of John McCrae's poem *In Flanders Fields* (P/O), the poppy became a symbol of the soldiers' sacrifice. It is used to this day when paper poppies are sold in November in aid of war veterans.

VERSIFICATION

The use of traditional and innovative metre and rhyme

The outbreak of the war brought a flood of patriotic poems employing conventional rhyme and metre (see Literary Terms) schemes. Rupert Brooke's *1914* sonnets are a model of this type of poem.

It cannot be said that the war brought about a breaking-up of the traditional moulds. Some of the best writing of the war (Blunden, Graves, Rosenberg, Sassoon, Morley, a good deal of Owen) continued to use traditional metrical and rhyme patterns. Moreover, there had been innovative poets well before the outbreak of the war, notably Gerard Manley Hopkins (1844–89) whose verse was published much later, in 1918. He used imperfect rhyme and sprung rhythm (see Literary Terms), and his work shows a desire for innovation (shared later by Owen, for instance) even though Hopkins could not influence the younger poets.

Largely, therefore, the form of these war poems was a matter of each poet's personal choice. As was said above, this was no literary 'school'. Nevertheless, the form of these war poems merits attention as well as the contents. To Wilfred Owen in particular, the form of his poems mattered greatly, and we can see in the earlier drafts of some of them how much thought he had given to their form. *Strange Meeting* in particular seems to have given him a lot of trouble. (His revisions may be found for instance in Jon Silkin's *Penguin Book of First World War Poetry* and in Edmund Blunden's edition of Owen's *Poems*.)

Note how the form of a poem can be crucial to its content.

Evidently Owen felt that assonance and pararhymes (see Literary Terms) had an important part to play in conveying the central metaphor (see Literary Terms) of the cave and its message. It may be that these poetical devices enhanced the image of the cave by their echoing sounds, or it may be that they created a subconscious feeling of dissatisfaction and unease (through the unexpected rhyming of vowels only in assonance and through the equally unexpected absence of the anticipated rhyme in pararhyme), which then contributed to the mood of despair. Whatever the reason, the form of the poem is crucial to its contents.

For that same reason perhaps the form of the verse changed as the war went on: free verse (see Literary Terms) came to be used more and more (by Sassoon, Rosenberg and Thomas in particular), and the images changed as well from the earlier abstractions of, say, Rupert Brooke to vivid, more concrete images.

Some of the poems, such as Isaac Rosenberg's *Dead Man's Dump*, would have lost their impact if confined to a formal rhyme scheme, not allowing the images to tumble out, horror upon horror. These images were not 'poetic', and neither could the form be.

PART FOUR

STUDY SKILLS

HOW TO USE QUOTATIONS

One of the secrets of success in writing essays is the way you use quotations. There are five basic principles:

- Put inverted commas at the beginning and end of the quotation
- Write the quotation exactly as it appears in the original
- Do not use a quotation that repeats what you have just written
- Use the quotation so that it fits into your sentence
- Keep the quotation as short as possible

Quotations should be used to develop the line of thought in your essays.

Your comment should not duplicate what is in your quotation. For example:

> **In *Recalling War* Robert Graves sees the war as a form of madness spreading across Europe. He says that it was 'an infection of the common sky'.**

Far more effective is to write:

> **In *Recalling War* Robert Graves sees the war hysteria as a fast-spreading disease, 'an infection of the common sky'**

Always lay out the lines as they appear in the text. For example:

> **Robert Graves sees the war as**
> **'No mere discord of flags**
> **But an infection of the common sky'.**

or:

> **Robert Graves sees the war as 'No mere discord of flags/But an infection of the common sky'.**

However, the most sophisticated way of using the writer's words is to embed them into your sentence:

> **By his use of the phrase 'an infection of the common sky' Robert Graves succeeds in establishing the dangerous nature of war hysteria and its prevalence across Europe.**

When you use quotations in this way, you are demonstrating your ability to use text as evidence to support your ideas.

Everyone writes differently. Work through the suggestions given here and adapt the advice to suit your own style and interests. This will improve your essay-writing skills and allow your personal voice to emerge.

The following points indicate in ascending order the skills of essay writing:

- Picking out one or two facts about the story and adding the odd detail
- Writing about the text by retelling the story
- Retelling the story and adding a quotation here and there
- Organising an answer which explains what is happening in the text and giving quotations to support what you write

....

- Writing in such a way as to show that you have thought about the intentions of the writer of the text and that you understand the techniques used
- Writing at some length, giving your viewpoint on the text and commenting by picking out details to support your views
- Looking at the text as a work of art, demonstrating clear critical judgement and explaining to the reader of your essay how the enjoyment of the text is assisted by literary devices, linguistic effects and psychological insights; showing how the text relates to the time when it was written

The dotted line above represents the division between lower and higher level grades. Higher-level performance begins when you start to consider your response as a reader of the text. The highest level is reached when you offer an enthusiastic personal response and show how this piece of literature is a product of its time.

Coursework essay

Set aside an hour or so at the start of your work to plan what you have to do.

- List all the points you feel are needed to cover the task. Collect page references of information and quotations that will support what you have to say. A helpful tool is the highlighter pen: this saves painstaking copying and enables you to target precisely what you want to use.
- Focus on what you consider to be the main points of the essay. Try to sum up your argument in a single sentence, which could be the closing sentence of your essay. Depending on the essay title, it could be a statement of the subject of the poem: 'In *Base Details* Sassoon paints a devastating picture of the incompetence and selfishness of the General Staff'; an opinion about setting: 'I think that the cave in Wilfred Owen's *Strange Meeting* is not Hell, as there is no suffering there, but rather the peace of the grave'; or a summary of the underlying theme: 'The main theme of Charlotte Mew's *The Cenotaph* is the waste of young lives in a war that has changed nothing for the better.
- Make a short essay plan. Use the first paragraph to introduce the argument you wish to make. In the following paragraphs develop this argument with details, examples and other possible points of view. Sum up your argument in the last paragraph. Check you have answered the question.
- Write the essay, remembering all the time the central point you are making.
- On completion, go back over what you have written to eliminate careless errors and improve expression. Read it aloud to yourself, or, if you are feeling more confident, to a relative or friend.

If you can, try to type your essay using a word processor. This will allow you to correct and improve your writing without spoiling its appearance.

Examination essay

The essay written in an examination often carries more marks than the coursework essay even though it is written under considerable time pressure.

In the revision period build up notes on various aspects of the text you are using. Fortunately, in acquiring this set of York Notes on *Poetry of the First World War*, you have made a prudent beginning! York Notes are set out to give you vital information and help you to construct your personal overview of the text.

Make notes with appropriate quotations about the key issues of the set texts. Go into the examination knowing your texts and having a clear set of opinions about them.

In most English Literature examinations you can take in copies of your set books. This in an enormous advantage although it may lull you into a false sense of security. Beware! There is simply not enough time in an examination to read the book from scratch.

In the examination

- Read the question paper carefully and remind yourself what you have to do.
- Look at the questions on your set texts to select the one that most interests you and mentally work out the points you wish to stress.
- Remind yourself of the time available and how you are going to use it.
- Briefly map out a short plan in note form that will keep your writing on track and illustrate the key argument you want to make.
- Then set about writing it.
- When you have finished, check through to eliminate errors.

To summarise, these are keys to success

- **Know the texts**
- **Have a clear understanding of and opinions on the setting, themes and writer's concerns**
- **Select the right material**
- **Plan and write a clear response, continually bearing the question in mind**

A typical essay question on *Poetry of the First World War* is followed by a sample essay plan in note form. This does not present the only answer to the question, merely one answer. Do not be afraid to include your own ideas and leave out some of the ones in this sample! Remember that quotations are essental to prove and illustrate the points you make.

Discuss the changing mood from enthusiastic patriotism to disillusionment, as reflected in the poetry of the First World War.

Part 1

Introduction. Mood of the early war years: either

- Enthusiastic patriotism (Hardy, *Men who March Away*; Binyon, *For the Fallen*) or
- The war as a chance to escape from boredom (Brooke, *Peace*)

Part 2

a) Causes of disillusionment:

- Unrealistic expectations of a brief and victorious war
- Ignorance of the nature of modern warfare
- Shock of the 1916 battles with their large numbers of casualties

b) Forms of disillusionment:

- Alienation from the people at home (Sassoon, *Blighters*, *Glory of Women*; Owen, *Dulce Et Decorum Est*)
- Horror (Blunden, *The Zonnebeke Road*; Owen, *The Sentry*; Rosenberg, *Dead Man's Dump*; Sassoon, *Suicide in the Trenches*, *Counter-Attack*; Graves, *The Dead Boche*)
- Pity for the dead and wounded (Owen, *Disabled*, *Mental Cases*, *Dulce Et Decorum Est*, *Anthem for Doomed Youth*, *Strange Meeting*; Rosenberg, *Dead Man's Dump*; Gurney, *The Silent One*, *To His Love*; Sassoon, *Suicide in the Trenches*)

- Anger against the incompetence of the High Command (Thomas, *This is No Case of Petty Right or Wrong*; Sassoon, *Base Details*, *The General*; Owen, *Strange Meeting)*

Part 3

The final years:

- Resignation (Thomas, *Lights Out*, *Rain*)
- Exhaustion – death as sleep (Owen, *Strange Meeting*, *Futility*, *Spring Offensive*; Blunden, *1916 seen from 1921*)
- Despair, fear of the future (Owen, *Strange Meeting;* Graves, *Recalling War*; Sassoon, *Does it Matter?*)

FURTHER QUESTIONS

Make a plan as shown above and attempt these questions.

1. Discuss the role of women in the war as reflected in the verse of two or three women writers of your choice.
2. It has been said that powerful emotions need powerful language. Discuss this statement with reference to the poetry of Wilfred Owen and Siegfried Sassoon, or Edmund Blunden and Robert Graves.
3. Write a letter from Wilfred Owen to Jessie Pope enclosing *Dulce Et Decorum Est* and explaining why you wrote it. You could even add Jessie Pope's reply!
4. Choose two or three poems illustrating men's opposing reactions when under threat of death – cowardice and great bravery – and discuss the treatment of these reactions in the poems of your choice.
5. In Wilfred Owen's *Anthem for Doomed Youth* do you see his choice of aural images for the first part and visual images for the second as deliberate? If so, how successful has he been in achieving his aim?
6. Does the poetry of the First World War reflect the class structure and cultural background of Edwardian England?

PART FIVE

CULTURAL CONNECTIONS

BROADER PERSPECTIVES

You have now read a short summary of the historical and social background to the war (Part One), studied the poems themselves with the help of the Summaries (Part Two), and become aware of some of the broader themes in the Commentaries (Part Three).

Novels of the First World War

Now it is time to look briefly at the poetry of the First World War from another angle. There is one aspect of this poetry that should be thought about: in no other European literature of that war is such a large body of poetry of such high order to be found.

In German literature one work stands out, Erich Maria Remarque's novel *Im Westen nichts neues* (Berlin, 1929). It was translated as *All Quiet on the Western Front* (Picador, 1987), and made into a film, directed by Lewis Milestone, in 1930.

In French literature it is again a novel that merits attention, Henri Barbusse's *Le Feu* (Paris, 1916). Translated as *Under Fire,* the novel is now out of print.

From central Europe came a sardonic epic by a Czech writer which goes some way to account for the collapse of the Austro-Hungarian empire: Jaroslav Hašek's *Osudy dobrého vojáka Švejka* (Prague, 1921–3). Translated as *The Good Soldier Schweik*, it is still in print in the Penguin edition (1939).

The First World War in other branches of English Literature

English literature also produced three remarkable autobiographies, all written by war poets: Edmund Blunden's *Undertones of War* (Penguin Modern Classics, 1982 – first published 1928), Robert Graves's *Goodbye to All That* (Penguin, 1990 – first published 1929) and Siegfried Sassoon's *Memoirs of an Infantry Officer* (Faber, 1965 – first published 1930).

If you are interested in women's experiences in the war, Vera Brittain's *Testament of Youth* (Arrow Books, 1960 – first published 1933) is a very useful source.

In the theatre R.C. Sherriff's *Journey's End* (1928) and Joan Littlewood's *Oh, What a Lovely War!* (1963) offer opposing views of the war, the patriotic versus the cynical and passionately pacifist. On television there was Baker's *Fatal Spring*, an imaginative reconstruction of the meeting of Graves, Owen and Sassoon at the Craiglockhart War Hospital in Edinburgh and, unexpectedly, the moving last episode of *Blackadder Goes Forth*.

Overall, however, there is nothing to touch the verse of the English war poets. We might try to explain this phenomenon by reference to the great tradition of lyrical poetry in English literature. Again, we might look for an explanation in the historical fact of a large number of educated, idealistic young men pitched into the horrors of the first modern war and finding in poetry a desperately needed means of expressing what they felt.

These are possible explanations for the appearance of the war poems but they do not explain their high quality and their extraordinary emotional appeal.

LITERARY TERMS

alliteration repetition of consonants at the beginning of a sequence of words
assonance rhyming of vowels only ('feel' and 'need')
dissonance disagreement, want of harmony
ellipsis grammatically incorrect omission of words (e.g. 'Who these hellish?' in Owen's *Mental Cases*)
euphemism use of a milder term to describe something unpleasant or offensive
foot section of a line of verse
free verse verse without any regular pattern of stresses and line lengths
half-rhyme imperfect rhyme (e.g. 'escaped' and 'scooped'). Also called a pararhyme
iambic referring to a foot of verse consisting of a weak stressed syllable followed by a strongly stressed one
iambic pentameter line of five iambic feet, the most common metre pattern in English verse. Unrhymed iambic pentameter, called blank verse, was used a great deal by Shakespeare
imagery language in which metaphors and similes are used. More generally, the word is used to cover all words appealing to the senses or feelings
imperfect rhyme see half-rhyme
metaphor figure of speech in which something is spoken of as being that which it resembles (e.g. 'Music showering', i.e. falling like rain, in Isaac Rosenberg's *Returning, We Hear the Larks*)
metre regulated succession of groups of syllables creating a pattern. It is based on the use of long and short or stressed and unstressed syllables
onomatopoeia use of words whose sound helps to suggest the meaning
oxymoron figure of speech which brings together two contradictory terms ('screaming dumbness' in Blunden's *The Zonnebeke Road*)
parable story with a hidden, usually moral meaning; Christ used parables in his teaching
pararhyme see **half-rhyme**
plot plan of a novel or a play. It should go beyond telling what has happened, and should suggest the basic pattern of interrelationships between the characters and between the events in the story
rhythm variation in the level of stress placed on syllables
simile poetic image which compares two things by pointing out the similarities between them. It should always contain the word 'as' or 'like'
sprung rhythm a rhythm pattern which is based on a fixed number of stressed syllables, taking no account of unstressed ones. This leads to an irregular number of feet per line
syntax arrangement of words in their proper grammatical forms and in the proper order, to express a meaning

TEST ANSWERS

TEST YOURSELF (p. 20)

1 *The Two Fusiliers* (Graves)
2 a soldier to his mate (Blunden, *Vlamertinghe*)
3 Edmund Blunden (*1916 seen from 1921*)
4 Rupert Brooke (*The Soldier*)
5 Stevens (Blunden, *The Zonnebeke Road*)
6 marching soldiers (Blunden, *Vlamertinghe*)

TEST YOURSELF (p. 40)

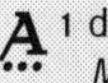

1 dead enemy soldier (Owen, *Strange Meeting*)
2 dying officer (Nichols, *Comrades*)
3 A.P. Herbert (*Beaucourt Revisited*)
4 Gurney's dead friend (*To His Love*)
5 Drummer Hodge (Hardy)
6 disabled soldier (Owen, *Disabled*)
7 the fighting man (Grenfell, *Into Battle*)

TEST YOURSELF (p. 51)

1 ploughman (Thomas, *As the Team's Head-Brass)*
2 Isaac Rosenberg *(Break of Day in the Trenches)*
3 coward's mother (Sassoon, *The Hero)*
4 Sassoon *(Base Details)*
5 the suicide (Sassoon, *Suicide in the Trenches)*
6 the general (Sassoon, *The General)*
7 dying man (Rosenberg, *Dead Man's Dump*)
8 Jesus and Barabbas (Sorley, *All the Hills and Vales Along*)

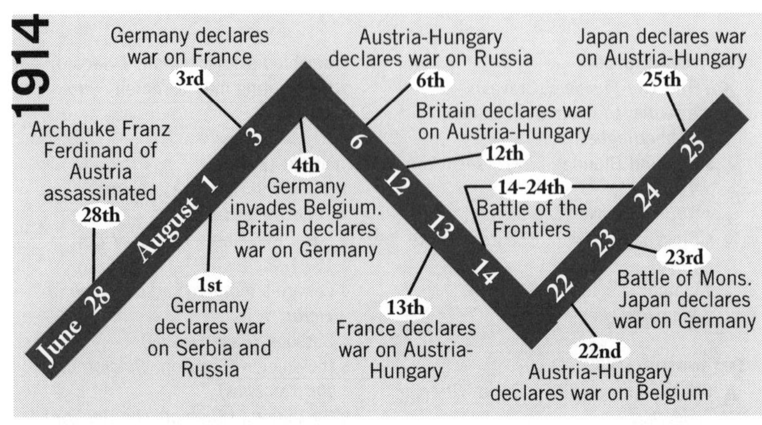
1914
Germany declares war on France
3rd
Austria-Hungary declares war on Russia
6th
Japan declares war on Austria-Hungary
25th
Archduke Franz Ferdinand of Austria assassinated
28th
Britain declares war on Austria-Hungary
12th
4th
Germany invades Belgium. Britain declares war on Germany
14-24th
Battle of the Frontiers
23rd
Battle of Mons. Japan declares war on Germany
1st
Germany declares war on Serbia and Russia
13th
France declares war on Austria-Hungary
22nd
Austria-Hungary declares war on Belgium
June 28
August 1
3
6
12
13
14
22
23
24
25

1915
Battle of Soissons
8-15th
Second Battle of Ypres. Germans introduce poison gas
22-25th
20th
R Brooke ✞
J Grenfell ✞
30th
15th
Battle of Festubert
January 8
15
April 20
22
30
May 15
25

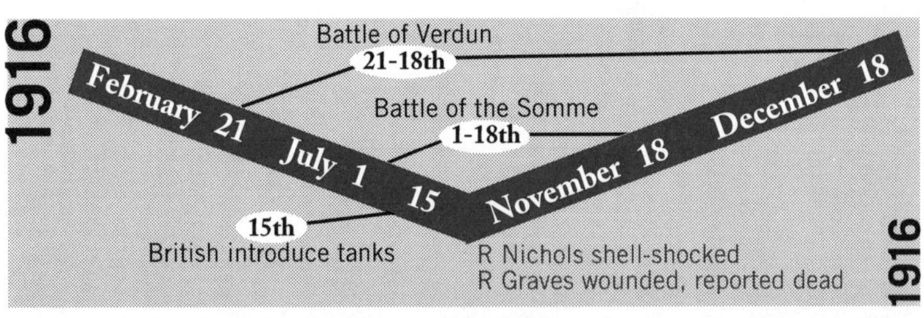
1916
Battle of Verdun
21-18th
Battle of the Somme
1-18th
15th
British introduce tanks
R Nichols shell-shocked
R Graves wounded, reported dead
February 21
July 1
15
November 18
December 18

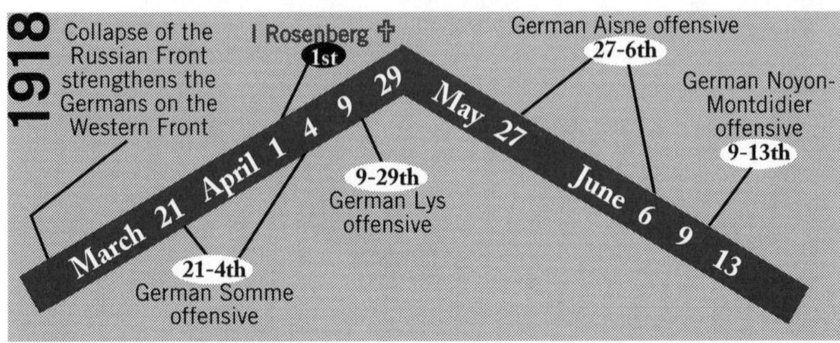
1918
Collapse of the Russian Front strengthens the Germans on the Western Front
I Rosenberg ✞
1st
German Aisne offensive
27-6th
German Noyon-Montdidier offensive
9-13th
9-29th
German Lys offensive
21-4th
German Somme offensive
March 21
April 1
4
9
29
May 27
June 6
9
13

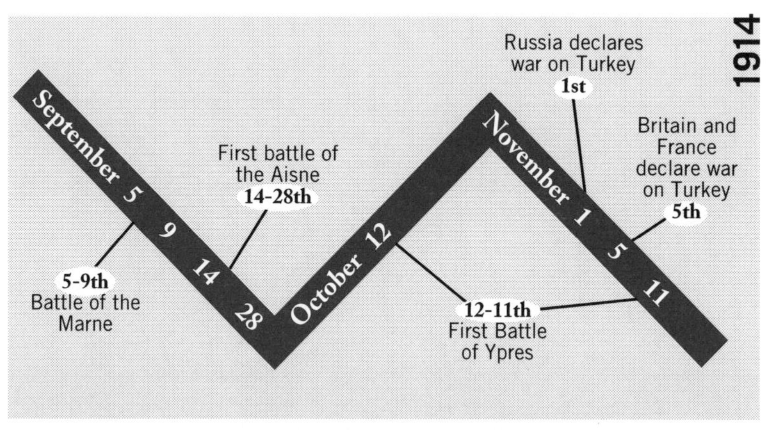
1914
September 5 9 14 28
October 12
November 1 5 11
Russia declares war on Turkey
1st
Britain and France declare war on Turkey
5th
First battle of the Aisne
14-28th
5-9th
Battle of the Marne
12-11th
First Battle of Ypres

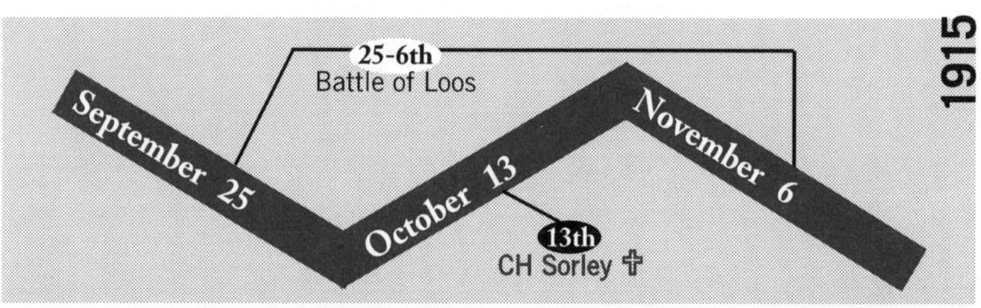
1915
September 25
October 13
November 6
25-6th
Battle of Loos
13th
CH Sorley ✝

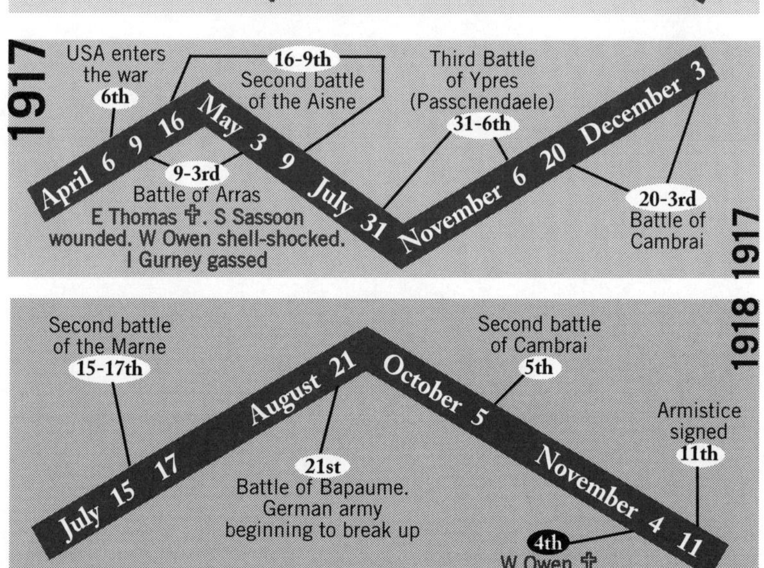
1917
April 6 9 16
May 3 9
July 31
November 6 20
December 3
USA enters the war
6th
16-9th
Second battle of the Aisne
Third Battle of Ypres (Passchendaele)
31-6th
9-3rd
Battle of Arras
E Thomas ✝. S Sassoon wounded. W Owen shell-shocked. I Gurney gassed
20-3rd
Battle of Cambrai
1917
1918
July 15 17
August 21
October 5
November 4 11
Second battle of the Marne
15-17th
Second battle of Cambrai
5th
Armistice signed
11th
21st
Battle of Bapaume. German army beginning to break up
4th
W Owen ✝

NOTES

FUTURE TITLES IN THE YORK NOTES SERIES

Chinua Achebe
Things Fall Apart

Edward Albee
Who's Afraid of Virginia Woolf?

Jane Austen
Mansfield Park

Jane Austen
Northanger Abbey

Jane Austen
Persuasion

Jane Austen
Sense and Sensibility

Samuel Beckett
Waiting for Godot

Alan Bennett
Talking Heads

John Betjeman
Selected Poems

Robert Bolt
A Man for All Seasons

Robert Burns
Selected Poems

Lord Byron
Selected Poems

Geoffrey Chaucer
The Franklin's Tale

Geoffrey Chaucer
The Merchant's Tale

Geoffrey Chaucer
The Miller's Tale

Geoffrey Chaucer
The Nun's Priest's Tale

Geoffrey Chaucer
Prologue to the Canterbury Tales

Samuel Taylor Coleridge
Selected Poems

Daniel Defoe
Moll Flanders

Daniel Defoe
Robinson Crusoe

Shelagh Delaney
A Taste of Honey

Charles Dickens
Bleak House

Charles Dickens
Oliver Twist

Emily Dickinson
Selected Poems

John Donne
Selected Poems

Douglas Dunn
Selected Poems

George Eliot
Middlemarch

George Eliot
The Mill on the Floss

T.S. Eliot
The Waste Land

T.S. Eliot
Selected Poems

Henry Fielding
Joseph Andrews

E.M. Forster
Howards End

E.M. Forster
A Passage to India

John Fowles
The French Lieutenant's Woman

Brian Friel
Translations

Elizabeth Gaskell
North and South

Oliver Goldsmith
She Stoops to Conquer

Graham Greene
Brighton Rock

Thomas Hardy
Jude the Obscure

Thomas Hardy
Selected Poems

Nathaniel Hawthorne
The Scarlet Letter

Ernest Hemingway
The Old Man and the Sea

Homer
The Iliad

Homer
The Odyssey

Aldous Huxley
Brave New World

Ben Jonson
The Alchemist

Ben Jonson
Volpone

James Joyce
A Portrait of the Artist as a Young Man

John Keats
Selected Poems

Philip Larkin
Selected Poems

D.H. Lawrence
The Rainbow

D.H. Lawrence
Sons and Lovers

D.H. Lawrence
Women in Love

Christopher Marlowe
Doctor Faustus

John Milton
Paradise Lost Bks I & II

John Milton
Paradise Lost IV & IX

Sean O'Casey
Juno and the Paycock

George Orwell
Nineteen Eighty-four

John Osborne
Look Back in Anger

Wilfred Owen
Selected Poems

Harold Pinter
The Caretaker

Sylvia Plath
Selected Works

Alexander Pope
Selected Poems

Jean Rhys
Wide Sargasso Sea

William Shakespeare
As You Like It

William Shakespeare
Coriolanus

William Shakespeare
Henry IV Pt 1

William Shakespeare
Henry V

William Shakespeare
Julius Caesar

William Shakespeare
Measure for Measure

William Shakespeare
Much Ado About Nothing

William Shakespeare
A Midsummer Night's Dream

William Shakespeare
Richard II

William Shakespeare
Richard III

William Shakespeare
Sonnets

William Shakespeare
The Taming of the Shrew

William Shakespeare
The Winter's Tale

George Bernard Shaw
Arms and the Man

George Bernard Shaw
Saint Joan

Richard Brinsley Sheridan
The Rivals

Muriel Spark
The Prime of Miss Jean Brodie

John Steinbeck
The Grapes of Wrath

John Steinbeck
The Pearl

Tom Stoppard
Rosencrantz and Guildenstern are Dead

Jonathan Swift
Gulliver's Travels

John Millington Synge
The Playboy of the Western World

W.M. Thackeray
Vanity Fair

Virgil
The Aeneid

Derek Walcott
Selected Poems

Oscar Wilde
The Importance of Being Earnest

Tennessee Williams
Cat on a Hot Tin Roof

Tennessee Williams
The Glass Menagerie

Virginia Woolf
Mrs Dalloway

Virginia Woolf
To the Lighthouse

William Wordsworth
Selected Poems

W.B. Yeats
Selected Poems